THE
PRINCESS
AND THE
DRAGON

THE
PRINCESS
AND THE
DRAGON

ROBERTO PAZZI

*Translated from the Italian
by M. J. Fitzgerald*

ALFRED A. KNOPF
New York
1990

THIS IS A BORZOI BOOK
PUBLISHED BY ALFRED A. KNOPF, INC.

Library of Congress Cataloging-in-Publication Data

Pazzi, Roberto, [date]
[Principessa e il drago. English]
The princess and the dragon / Roberto Pazzi.
p.   cm.
Translation of: *La principessa e il drago.*
ISBN 0-394-57255-6
Fiction.   I. Title.
PQ4876.A98P7513   1990
853'.914—dc20   89-43380
CIP

Manufactured in the United States of America

FIRST EDITION

To E.

Foreword

GEORGE ALEXANDROVICH ROMANOV is one of Tsar Nicholas's brothers. So little is known about him that I hope the reader will forgive a plundering of the imagination at the expense of historical fact. I found a vague mention of his death in Osip Mandelstam's *The Clamour of Time*. I became enthusiastic when the street lamps were covered in black crepe and tied with black ribbon on the occasion of the heir to the throne's funeral.

The Grand Duke died of tuberculosis the 28th of June 1899 in the Caucasus mountains. Well-sheltered in his century, he was the only one of the last generation of the Romanovs to be buried in the Cathedral of Sts. Peter and Paul in Petersburg, where by pure chance I found him, next to his father, Alexander III, on a trip to the Soviet Union after I had written his imaginary story.

ROBERTO PAZZI

Ferrara, February 1986

THE
PRINCESS
AND THE
DRAGON

Prologue

HIS Holiness was taking a stroll in the garden of the Apostolic Palace one autumn Sunday afternoon; that day the Cardinal Archbishops of Madrid and Warsaw had been to lunch. Here I sit, between the opposites of Europe, the venerable Pontiff had thought at one point during the meal, when the discussion among his guests had grown heated. The old prelate from Andalusia would be taking back to the King of Spain permission for the closing of a number of monasteries reduced to a few lay brothers and already on the verge of extinction. The Polish Primate was on his way to Warsaw with a warm invitation on the part of the Pope that the Tsar, Sovereign of Poland, respect the right to Catholic education in Polish schools.

His Holiness walked slowly in the golden light along the avenue, leaning on the silver walking stick that had belonged to Madame Mère, the mother of Napoleon and friend of an uncle of the Pope; she had died in Rome sixty years before and the walking stick had passed to Eustorgio Pecci, Bishop of Cagli and Pergola. Sometimes as he leaned on it, the old Pontiff considered by what strange channels the chattels of history reached posterity; he had jokingly remarked to Monsignor Aldobrandini that leaning on Letizia's staff made him feel he was not only Father but Mother to all Catholics. "A very interesting theological concept—yes, indeed it is, and worthy of examination, Your Holiness," the domestic prelate had been quick to concur in his high-pitched voice. "My dear Monsignor, I'm much too old to examine; I'll gladly leave the whole concept to my successor. I'm content to lean on the staff," the Pontiff had replied, looking at the silver handle.

But on this autumn day there were considerations in his mind utterly different from the motherhood of God, completely different thoughts . . . the Polish business, above all. That blessed man, the Cardinal of Warsaw, had made such strange remarks. They really did not want him to die in peace, to close his eyes on an untroubled Christianity, free of controversy . . . but did he not have a right to it at ninety? He had been at the helm of the Church for twenty years, guiding the battered ship of Peter, which he had inherited in such a poor state from Pius, steering it through storms and past the shallows of these present times.

All the sovereigns who had accepted democracy, who had cooperated to spread the contemporary pragmatism that undermined the very roots of power—what harm they had done to the heart of the Church! Another Leo had halted the Huns as they were about to descend upon Rome and vandalize the Church, but the effort on his own part, the thirteenth Pope to bear the glorious and militant name, had by no means been less, having to withstand the hordes of materialists of this century.

And now, beloved Poland, entangled in the woof of a foreign power for more than a century, driven to practice its Christian and Roman rites almost in secret. How disturbing were the proposals made in an attempt to avoid violent rebellion and loss of life, what burdensome diplomatic maneuvers awaited him and the state secretariat! The Polish Cardinal had spoken of the creation of a separate Polish kingdom, with one of the Tsar's brothers as Sovereign: young Grand Duke George Alexandrovich, described as a mystic, a bit of a dreamer, troubled by a sensibility heightened by consumption; very little else was known of him. Assuming even that Poland agreed to an arrangement that would give it this kind of autonomy, would Nicholas II agree to separate Poland from the other states under his dominion? And, would the Grand Duke leave the nation free to practice its religion?

The Cardinal of Warsaw was insistent on the ambition of the Prince Grand Duke. And there was also an underlying conflict with the Grand Duke's brother, a marriage to which the Tsar was opposed and which he persisted in preventing because of the illness.

"What happens if the poor Prince dies young, since he is already so ill?" asked the Pope.

"Your Holiness, that is precisely why we wish him to father some children as soon as possible," the Cardinal had coolly replied.

"Easier to say, Your Eminence . . . and if by some mischance the Princess you spoke of were to be infertile?"

5

"The information I have testifies to her being very healthy, very energetic, an ideal mother."

But the Holy Father remained unconvinced. To place a consumptive on the throne of a puppet kingdom, with the immediate duty of fathering children with a cousin in a marriage that would alienate his brother, to then be left free to die really did not seem the best solution to him. Besides, twenty years of Vatican diplomacy had not changed him completely: he felt sorry for that young man.

When the Cardinal Archbishop of Madrid, the other guest at the table, had been asked his opinion on the delicate question, he replied, without lifting his eyes from the partridge on his plate, that in his country they knew nothing of such matters, that in Spain they were free of such political machinations, thank God.

He wants something from the Pope, the Archbishop of Warsaw had thought as he continued to explain.

When the Spanish Cardinal ventured to say how lucky it was that his King had no siblings, however, the Polish Cardinal could contain himself no longer: "Carlism was not invented by us, and your Bourbons have caused more wars of succession than any other royal family."

"Are you defending the Romanovs now? Have you forgotten the blood treaty betwen Alexander I and Constantine, behind his poor father's back?" the Spaniard had immediately retaliated.

The opposites of Europe, here they are . . . never again at the same table, never ever again, Leo had thought, taking the last sip of the precious Tuscan wine.

"My very dear Eminences, I beg of you, let's leave to God all judgment on the potentates of the earth. I did not call you to pass judgment, and the time of the Areopagites is long past. . . ."

Later, in the private library, the Spanish Cardinal had turned to his younger colleague with a courtesy that had been appreciated even by the old Pontiff: "Well, in Rome there are people who know the young Grand Duke George, if you need to find out more about him, gain certain information about his character. The Infanta Maria Eulalia was telling me just last week in Madrid about a friendship between Prince Victor Emmanuel and the brother of the Tsar; they've corresponded for years, they share a passion for coin collecting. One could approach the Prince of Naples, despite the problems there are at the moment . . ."

"Yes, with those Philistine Savoyards."

"And yet, Your Eminence, some sign of good will has reached us from the Royal Family, especially since the marriage of the Crown Prince with Helen of Montenegro," the Pope observed.

"Yes, yes, the news even reached us in Poland—the blue-blooded shepherdess."

"She is the most pious and gentle Princess in the Savoy family, apart from the good Clotilda. I have great hopes that she will succeed in softening those hard-necked Piedmontese. I shall try and approach Victor Emmanuel through her and find out what kind of person the Grand Duke is."

Now, walking in the Vatican gardens, the Pope thought back to the question and felt a growing anger with the Polish people: ". . . This vocation they have for martyrdom . . . we know how they are, these Poles who every thirty years or so have to rise up and die to defend their faith, or their country, or their king, or because they have no

7

king; they can never suffer in silence, they have to scream out their pain as if they were the only ones subjected to the violence of dominion by a foreign power. They have not pondered Saint Augustine to any depth; too often they demand justice here, in the Civitas Terrena. Sometimes they remind me of my young seminarians in Perugia when I heard their confessions—what is it, sixty years ago; can it be? They were so involved with their own troubles, so convinced they were the only ones to endure them; certainly they were different from everyone else . . . top of the class, my Poles, first in class, so exquisitely intolerable. . . ."

SOME time later, links were finally made between the Holy See and the House of the Prince of Naples. A thick and detailed report on talks between the Italian Prince and Cardinal Cornaggia-Medici, a prelate close to the Royal Family, was brought to the ailing Pontiff, now confined to an armchair.

Sitting by the window, his head against the back of the chair, his hands unmoving in his lap, the Pope gazed at the sky. The piscatory ring was so loose around the finger deformed by arthritis that it was as if it had been removed from a much larger hand. The January sky was of that mild Roman-winter blue barely distinguishable from the gray of the low clouds. Drowsy and indifferent clouds, stretching out so low before his eyes. . . ; it was as if they wanted to bring the city blessed so often by him into a contact with the sky different from the one he was contemplating.

. . . Rome has remained as it was twenty years ago, no less cynical, no less indifferent. I have not been a good

Bishop. The scandals, the corruption of these last years run through it like a sewer. Now I know why Peter made his seat in Rome: Rome swallows everything; its very spiritual rottenness guarantees the survival of all faiths, all orders, all empires, every regime and every monarchy. Its workings have never deceived me: it killed Caesar, Peter and Cola; it drove out and received Pius back with identical lightheartedness. Already they are preparing solemn rites for my funeral with the same superficial awe with which they'll welcome my successor. This is not merely a city, this is a world; the WORLD is reflected in this, the WORLD as a hellhole. . . . But I, I am at the end, my Lord. My wish has been granted: you call me, you lift me, away from this vale of tears where only death reigns. . . .

And the old Lion lowered his head, looked at the ring, that ring that would be broken. His eyes then fell on the leather folder next to his armchair: the report on the young Russian Prince. . . . How distant, how increasingly foreign and alien that vain politicking seemed.

Yet it had to be dealt with, to the final breath; he was still Father of all believers. The Poles expected a comforting word from him: his most difficult children. His thoughts returned to the Cardinal of Warsaw, the last talks, the growing tension between Russia and Poland, the inconclusive exchanges with Tsar Nicholas II. He opened the folder and began to read the beautiful Latin of Cardinal Cornaggia-Medici, one of the last humanists in the Holy See. After a delightfully composed prologue about his regal intermediary, the Prince of Naples, whom God had granted a spouse "*tam pulchra et pia*"—well, well, Cornaggia-Medici, you remain a great socialite, despite the purple—the prelate

9

began his portrait of Grand Duke George Alexandrovich, second son of Alexander III.

However weak and exhausted the old Pope felt, his curiosity was aroused as he read on. Perhaps the Prince of Naples did not have an exact idea of the Russian Prince, perhaps they had only spoken of ancient brass farthings and ducats, for it wasn't possible that such a man existed in Russia. As a child, he had shown signs of a highly Protestant vocation by a strong sensitivity to the question of predestination. But how then could the love story with his cousin be explained, a story so delicately perfumed with idealism, in a man who was said to aspire to an awareness of life as a disease that only death would cure? Because it was clear that the young Grand Duke had distinguished himself from his brothers by an aberrant and precocious attraction for death.

The man described here is a real Catholic Prince; he is neither young, nor Russian, nor Orthodox, the Pope thought as he read. He learned details of the journey of the Tsar's children to Asia—the grand tour through Egypt to the East—in a narrative whose delicacy could only be compared to a spoken confession, and he saw more and more clearly that the man was not the right sovereign for the Poles. A man of such ancient sensibility could not reign over young colts, could never love them; nor would they understand a king of such keen intelligence and awareness, such disillusion coupled with tragic idealism. He could have reigned in Spain, at the opposite end of Europe, immediately after Philip II, the Pope thought.

The Cardinal explained at the end of the report that highly confidential information had come from sources other

than the Prince of Naples, whose wife had told him that
the Khedive of Egypt might know more. Helen had not
always lived among the shepherds of Cetinje; she and her
sisters Militza and Anastasia had spent many years in Petersburg; they knew many things. . . .

No, George was not cut out to be King of Poland. And
Pope Leo XIII wearily closed the folder, leaned his head
against the back of the chair and looked at the sky once
more, where a curiously shaped dot in the clouds gave the
impression of a bird in flight. He did not notice that the
daguerrotype of the Grand Duke had slid from the folder
to the carpet and was suddenly lifted in a gust of air as at
that moment the door opened.

It's more likely to be the carriage of the devil flying
through the air, the Pontiff thought. It's more likely this
Prince will die young, he's so in love with death . . . he'd
have made a good Pope. . . .

I

WAITING

1

GEORGE, brother to Tsar Nicholas II, was sitting in his armchair one December morning with a cup of tea in his hand. The slender wrists trembled slightly against the cuffs of his silk dressing gown.

More and more frequently, a fever coursed through him in waves while he let himself be shaved, while he washed, picked out a tie, waistcoat, shirt, cuff links. It took him at least two hours. Two hours to adorn and show forth his royal body. He did not always feel like dressing and leaving his rooms in the castle at Livadia, the place where his illness had kept him confined for the last two years.

To dress for others seemed to him among the most real causes of his disease; he was aware that his waking led to an inevitable, perfectly rehearsed series of actions on the part of a dozen or so people in some wing of the palace, actions choreographed by the adjutant Prince Ourousov. By being late, it was possible to delay the actions by a few hours, but the requirements of the play had to be respected. Otherwise there might be a visit from St. Petersburg by the Empress Mother, not something to wish for. Her eyes would give him the strength to sustain the futile and tiring audiences for a couple of days, to take on parts that illness had allowed him to drop, but then he would plunge into an even deeper dejection, an even greater fatigue and listlessness. Nicholas at least could derive some kind of satisfaction from his personal annihilation: he was Tsar. But no one else in the Imperial family could be rescued from an existence halfway between Tsar and subject, the sensation of living in a no-man's-land without shape or identity, prey to an unease that seemed to him more and more destined to end in long, unconscious sleep.

As soon as he awoke he began to wait; there was a lot of time to waste in front of the Crimean Sea. Like a relentless fly, the consciousness of waiting buzzed in George's ear; he tried to crush it against the tall glass window that gave onto the sea, and, facing all that blue, he felt as if he had stopped it. But it escaped, slid under the yellow paper of Helen's last letter, which he read again and again like the waves of his fever. For a while the Grand Duke would forget what lay around him and would again see Helen's face, with its straight stubborn line above the beautiful nose that so many members of her mother's family shared. Helen must come to him; against the will of all the family she must come to him there—and soon, if she was still to find him. He should warn Ourousov to order a maid to take fresh flowers every morning to the rooms the Princess would be occupying. How could he not have thought of it before?

Helen liked marigolds, those yellow flowers with stems

of such crude bright green, a violent green that could not last in full bloom more than a few days. How could he find those flowers? Other flowers were content with a less intense color, a more subdued green in different shades; other flowers blossomed all the year round, and she did not like them so much because they could be found everywhere. Where could marigolds be found beyond their brief flowering? How could he rescue this woman from her claim to be living without waiting, without memory, for the moment, unconnected to the world? She had been the one who had taught him to be indifferent on those mornings when he did not care to dress for others; she had been the one to set the example of intolerance toward the rules of a game so often so alien. Yes, perhaps Nicholas could represent for the Russians everything that was sacred in that immense and savage land through the adornment of his very body by uniforms. George's sloth, his melancholy came from his thirst to live through Helen; he could not protect himself from such deathly desire except with the plea of a disease, an alibi taken so seriously that the lie had become truth and the illness had really taken root. The times when he was better, without fever, he felt as if he wandered among the members of the small court forgetful of some very important thing, absentminded and bewildered again by the titles and forms with which the nothing bedecks itself: the Highnesses, the Excellencies that surrounded him, the messages from the Sovereign his brother, the letters from his sister-in-law the Tsarina, the service orders sent by the regiment.

Because it was necessary to pretend to be well in the presence of the family, of officers and soldiers, of servants and the subjects who in Crimea testified to the Empire of his father and his brother, George did not think of the future. He knew there was no future for the Empire, only an eternal present, an eternal waiting as in hell. Hell was waiting: he had experienced it so exactly in life that he could no longer expect it in death if death should, after all, be mysterious. But he felt death to be a mistress without secrets; he knew her so well, and his knowledge had frayed her so. Helen had to come; even if it were to be forbidden, he could no longer wait. . . . At their last meeting, during a religious ceremony in Zagorsk, she had spoken to him from behind a column, whispered of Cannes where cousin Militza had a villa: "Shall we go there by land or by sea, my love?" As if the only problem were practical, by train, by boat. That the Tsar opposed them, that he, George, was ill and her father did not want her to sacrifice her life—all this was secondary, questions that could wait another time.

He had prepared for their trip for weeks now, running through timetables and other information brought to him by the adjutant. And of course Ourousov pretended to go along with his wishes, but kept George's brother fully informed. Ourousov's devotion had perimeters that corresponded exactly to the pomp and circumstance of his life: one was an Imperial Grand Duke only because there was an Emperor, and the adjutant conformed just as much to this ineluctable law, his own existence justified by the existence of the Tsar. Ourousov acted well; a different behavior would have been suspect, might have been evidence of a treason inspired by an inconceivable apprehension of equality between people. Helen alone could escape the rules of the game, be the exception, interrupt the waiting by breaking the pattern of impersonal devotion, busy herself with trains, departures for France, invent a different death, one with as great a seductive mystery as life itself. Let the doctors come and tell him that the only suitable climate for him, for his illness, was the climate of Crimea; Helen had told him of a house where he could live in Cannes— outside Russia, far from his brother, beyond the reach of the Empire.

It was clear that he could not take everything to his new life abroad; he spent whole days drawing up alternative lists of those items that would follow him, discovering what he could give up. Time taught the lesson of separation from objects: he had only to think how accustomed he had become to separation from the people, to their disappearance from his life; and so, looking at the books, the coin collection, Uncle Nicholas's swords, clothes, ties, George gradually learned detachment from them.

At night the journey loomed nearer than by day, and one night he had taken down suitcases and trunks himself and begun to pack, as if it were a dress rehearsal. But even while he opened drawers and filled the suitcases, he realized he was bringing items to them that he then took back to the drawers. At dawn he saw that he had barely enough to fill one piece of luggage. Later he thought that if he had stayed up, if sleep had not overtaken him and interrupted the packing, he would have reached the conclusion that not even these few clothes were essential to his journey with Helen. He would have to ask her when he got there: those who live always in Russia, especially the brother of a Tsar, could not know how life might be on the coast of that other sea. She had asked him if he wanted to go by sea; it would be wonderful to leave from the harbor of Livadia, to abandon his home and the Empire, see them disappear beyond the horizon at sunset when the light diminishes slowly, when night falls and the lights of the castle are all lit. And for once those lights would not go on because he was in there, a prisoner unable to enter the wonderful outside world: it would be someone else who would see the windows lit up, would take note of the signal, make the sortie he had so often made; someone else would save him from the fear of not being seen and perhaps mistaken for a stranger as he stood looking up and recognizing his own windows where the lights had just been lit.

He would leave with his rescuers and never return. If he could shed his life of suffering in Russia like the hide of the beast in the fairy tale, and merely remember it, he thought he could even learn to love it. He laughed thinking of what they might say at court, in the government, in the drawing rooms of St. Petersburg, imagining the faces of the courtiers, of the adjutant. The brother of the Tsar, that sick one, the one who lives year in and year out in the warmth of Crimea, has eloped abroad with his cousin. . . . But perhaps he deceived himself and no one would notice; breaking the rules of the game was no guarantee of attention. Their reaction concerned him as little as the chatter of the servants in the garden, where the chauffeur and the head gardener had spent the last half hour discussing the problems of sending flowers to the capital, by train, for the Tsarina. Roses, her favorite flower.

He would call Ourousov; he wanted his mail and to ask about the doctor. As he stretched his left hand to the bell,

George noticed it, white, restless, but free of the blue veins that crisscrossed his right hand. Now he saw the right hand as Helen had seen it, so shaky it saddened her each time she took it in her hands. Did she see some kind of premonition in the pale nerve-ridden hand? He would know it abroad, when he reached Cannes for that new life. How he would like to have had a previous life, some episode, some event that he could lay at the altar of that absolute love as a sacrificial offering, to deepen it, make it grow as it exerted its force on the new life of the other . . . to be able to offer the long silence that weighs down, heavy as sin; to be able to say that yes, he had known secrecy and deceit—how much better would that have been for their love! But there was nothing to summon forth, there was no other life in his life, there was no secret door that could spring open, no skeleton that could appear after many years: only his short life, his uncertain health. And if the imagination was to stop filling the cracks, put an end to all justification, if the imagination was to stop working to help flesh out his life, how could he induce it to continue? It was not possible to end the fairy tale with an "and they lived happily ever after": he had no past to hide. Even if he had, there is no past that love cannot justify and redeem. He would have to pledge another area of his life, the future. And beyond the future his eternity, where only a superhuman force greater even than love could save him with an endless redemption. All he could do was wait for Helen, who had this strength of love.

He pulled the bell cord. A few minutes later Prince Ourousov came in with letters and told him the doctor was waiting in the antechamber. And George sank slowly into the rituals that made him long for solitude and night: invitations from the notables of the area, service orders from the regiment on military maneuvers in the Caucasus, the little letters of his younger sisters, Xenia and Olga, the proofs of the coin catalogue to correct, letters from that other royal coin collector, the Prince of Naples.

While the doctor rummaged his flesh looking for some development in the disease to barter as an improvement, George stared at a patch on the ceiling and noticed how the composition of Mars and Venus was being reshaped in a new and disturbing way by the shadow of dampness moving across the pink flesh of love. He turned to look out of the window as the doctor felt his pulse; his friend the sea, so clear, so real, as bright as the green of Helen's marigolds, brought him back down to earth. Why did she ask him whether by sea or land? Wasn't there in fact only one way? He had studied hendiadys, single expressions, as a boy in ancient Latin textbooks, "*terra marique*," by land and sea. There was nothing to choose; there was choice only in the very refusal to choose, just as land is both the starting point and the end of every journey by sea.

"Imperial Highness, a walk today would do you good." The doctor had been glancing at him since he had turned to look out of the window. Had he not understood that the garden was no longer enough? He too, like everyone else, was ready to reduce things to the lowest common denominator to ensure contentment. Certainly there was a stand-in for Helen somewhere, probably ready to marry him if he could compromise. If only he were less strange, less extravagant, calmer, less demanding, there was, in his mother's mind, in his brother's plans, in the letters from Xenia and Olga, a whole life laid out for him: a wife.

The doctor dictated to Ourousov the medicines of the day while the servant came in to take orders for the kitchen. "Cold but nourishing foods" was the doctor's prescription. The Prince continued to write, and the Grand Duke thought how many people through the years had taken trouble over his body. He tried to picture the line of servants, valets, cooks, coachmen, butlers, gardeners; he remembered the half-empty suitcase to which all his luggage could be reduced. Who of all his retinue was he to take? And he was reminded of tombs into which ancient Asian civilizations lowered the furnishings and slaves of kings—was it Ashurbanipal? He remembered a painting: the slaying of the king's favorites around the dying sovereign.

But he himself was not going to be conquered by illness; he would escape with Helen, he was going to win! There was a gateway down there, through the strait he would need to cross from the sea of Livadia to reach that other sea, where France was, where his new home was. And there, there too, there was another gateway, a gateway to reach the ocean, to reach the Americas. . . . Whenever he thought of the journey, he let himself get lost in the details: the name of the ship, the time of departure of the train, the joint surname they would use at various frontiers.

The latest news of Helen had come in a letter from Xenia, the sister to whom he had been closer during the last years in St. Petersburg. He had to reach Helen directly, without untrustworthy intermediaries like Ourousov, or intermediaries with little cunning and less freedom like his sister. But others listened on the telephones both in St. Petersburg and here in Livadia; he was a prisoner of his own court, each member as ready to betray him as the adjutant. No one in the Imperial family was truly free, but to him had fallen the thicker bars of illness. Despite the sunny winter morning and the heavy coat, he shivered with fever when he went into the garden with Prince Ourousov. He walked slowly toward the sloops of the Imperial yacht: that morning the funnels of the *Standard* were smoking; the captain must have decided to test some of the engines. Perhaps he would see the black ship take to the sea. He drew near a bench and sat, dismissing Ourousov with a wave of the hand. He had understood early that he was different from the rest of his family, that he could not live as his older brother did.

On the other great journey of his life, with the Tsarevich his brother, they had gone by sea; it was not true he had not seen the world. It had been a long journey through the East, to discover Russia's two great sleeping sisters, India and China.

2

ALEXANDER III had wanted a long educational trip for his sons that would avoid a Europe torn apart by class struggles and by the formation of parliaments in monarchies that had begun to crumble as they accepted the rules of democracy. He wanted his sons to delight in the vastness of Asia; he wanted them to learn to take pleasure in their destiny as sovereigns of a land where every journey was calculated in walking days, where one man's will was law. They left from St. Petersburg in October, 1890, on board the Russian cruiser *Pamiat Azora*, waved at from the shore by the Tsar and the Tsarina. The Tsar was radiant that his boys were leaving to receive the homage of the world, in countries where preparations were already under way to greet the sons of the Russian autocrat suitably. The Tsarina was worried, apprehensive for her delicate sons, especially George, so tall and thin, so pale, so worn by consumption. A few weeks earlier, there had been the final verdict: it was undoubtedly tuberculosis.

Before they climbed on board, Alexander and Maria held their sons in their arms: George still remembered his father's words to Nicholas: "Not even the son of the Emperor of China will reign as you are to reign. You have no need to leave Russia. I send you simply for enjoyment, nothing more." And their mother looked long and hard, did not speak for fear of crying and seemed not to see Nicholas, she was so focused on George in the white uniform of the Imperial Navy. He was nineteen, and his mother was bestowing on him a consciousness of death; her eyes told him that he might not return from this journey. And while the cruiser, pulled by the towing vessels, slowly left the wharf where the Imperial court pressed around his father, he saw everything gradually become smaller: the white villas, the breakwaters of the harbor, the long warships, the steeples with their golden crosses, the senate building, the high spires of SS. Peter and Paul, the cathedral where his grandfather slept.

And he saw the figure of Alexander III, Emperor and autocrat of all Russias—Tsar of Moscow, Vladimir, Novgorod, Kazan', Astrakhan, Poland, Siberia, Kerchensky, Poluostrovnoy and Georgia; Lord of Pskov; Grand Duke of Smolensk, Lithuania, Vol'dino, Podolsk and Finland; Prince of Estonia, Livny, Kurilovka, Sen'kovo, Samara, Bialystok, Kareliy, Tvayan, Yugorskij, Perm, Viavatn and Bulgaria; Lord and Grand Duke of Novgorod the Lower, Cernik, Peza, Polotsk, Rostov, Yaroslavskaya, Belozer'ye, Udova, Oblivskaya, Vitebsk, Mstislavl' and of all the regions of the North; Lord and Sovereign of the lands of

Ikanovka, Kartayël, Kabardino-Balkarskaya and of the provinces of Armenia; Sovereign of the Princes of Circassia
and the Princes of the Mountain; Duke of Schleswig-Hol-
stein, Stormovo, of the Sitmar and Oldenburg; Lord of
Turkestan, heir to Norway—become smaller and smaller,
until he vanished altogether.

He stayed on deck looking for a long time, long after
St. Petersburg had vanished and Russia was nothing more
than a strip of blue slightly darker than the blue of the sea.
But he could see the roads, the squares, the bridges, the
acetylene light of streetlamps, the slender golden steeple
of the Admiralty with the two wrought-iron anchors on
either side of the gateway on the Neva, the Imperial flag
on the tower of the fortress of SS. Peter and Paul; and his
father, in Catherine's vast study at the Gatchina Palace,
sitting at the immense oak desk neatly stacked with red
folders from ministers, his pen racing on the page, halting
Time in Cyrillic script.

The two young Grand Dukes were not alone on that
trip. Alexander had wanted the élite scions of the aristocracy
to keep his two eldest company. Amongst others were
Prince Baviatinsky, Prince Obolensky and Prince Oukh-
tomsky. When the ship reached Piraeus, the only European
port in which they dropped anchor, the two brothers en-
thusiastically welcomed cousin George, son of the King of
Greece, and the real trip began: George was the liveliest
of the princes of Europe. After he joined them, there was
no peace on board ship: cards, dice, champagne filled the
time between stops in the warmest and most entertaining
cities of Egypt. Long nights on the Nile began, on the
yacht of the Khedive, to which the Egyptian ruler had

welcomed his royal guests from Europe. And in that kingdom undone by sweet and wanton memories, they followed the young Greek Prince, daring and spoilt, irresistible in his gaiety, through the worst areas of the muddy cities. The two Russian cousins saw in their Greek relative the soul of their Asian origins, the other head of the two-headed eagle. Following him, they forgot who they were; they never knew that the Egyptian police were posted behind the doors, beyond the walls of the secret chambers, just beyond the beds, present at every acknowledged and unacknowledged pleasure. They never knew that the Khedive received a detailed report every morning, with each moment of their nights accounted for, and that the corpulent ruler had enjoyed reading it, smiling at the innocence of the princes. Only one detail had touched him, a gesture by the younger of the Russian Grand Dukes, who, before leaving a dancer at dawn, had caressed her for a long time to put her to sleep in order that she not notice his departure. And before, during the night, how passionate he had been. When they are so passionate, they are conscious of death, the Khedive had thought, remembering a beautiful brother of his who had died of consumption in Cannes; the Queen Mother carried the portrait of that young face in a locket around her neck, and never took it off.

When the moment of departure for India came, the Khedive gave each of his guests a precious keepsake. He waited to hand over the gift to the Tsar's second son until the crowd had dispersed, and while the dignitaries were taking leave of the other princes, he handed him the jade statuette of a dancer from the royal treasury, the gift of an Arabian caliph to the Khedive's grandfather.

"This Egypt bestows on thee," the Khedive had said in his own language. George, startled, looked into those flashing black eyes and felt the enigmatic and purposeful gaze pierce through him. He lowered his eyes, clasping the jade dancer. But his composure returned quickly, and he thanked the ruler in faultless French. The Khedive resumed his usual apathetic mien and answered in the same language, wishing him a good journey through all the beautiful lands he still had to visit.

Later, on the cruiser, as the ship took to sea, the cousin, a good Greek, could not contain his dislike of that "fat pig," the Khedive. "Look, look what he gave me, look," he said, and showed the company an alabaster vase whose ambiguous shape could have been a woman but also a boy. "Ah, the Turks, they have only one obsession, my friends," he added.

George looked at the statuette, saw again the young Egyptian woman asleep and for the first time felt a dislike for his Greek cousin. He withdrew to his cabin and took up the book he had started to read at the beginning of the cruise, *The Thousand and One Nights*, and refused to come out. Each of the young people on board was gripped by the frenzy of being adult, it seemed to him; the visits and the lewd entertainments were nothing more than a way to kill time between the present and the moment when most of them would inherit power, or riches, or a father's titles. The journey seemed like a dull wait in an antechamber, with his friends greedy to enter, kill their youth, reach maturity. It was not a real trip. He did not like the pleasure of this kind of killing; he knew better than his companions what it was like to be young and know oneself already old.

The women he had encountered so far on the journey had revealed it to him, recognizing in every embrace the sign of an early regret. In one night the dancer had been his companion through the many years of lives he would never live, had shown him that she was not one woman, but many women from different ages. Exhausted, she had whispered to him before dawn, "Enough now, Prince. There are no more lives," and had lain back, light, on the bed. And in that fraction, at the closing of the eyelids, she had taken on the many centuries of her land and become ageless. And he had returned to being the boy who had left Russia for the first time, bearing with him a fever.

Love on that first occasion had been consciousness of a thousand other selves, as if he had entered a dark room and gained confidence by feeling the objects, the furnishings; many of those selves had by now dropped by the wayside, and he had lost the memory of them. He realized that night, still in Egypt, that he had lost the violent George, the boy who hankered for swords, firearms, any gun; he had lost another George, eager to frighten his younger sisters by hiding far from the nanny's eyes along the dark passages of the Anitchkov Palace; and still another one, at Spala, shuddering for hours on end in contemplation of the large portrait of his mother in ceremonial dress, with sapphires gleaming on the satin skin. Now, on this December morning in front of the sea of Livadia, he remembered their arrival in Bombay, the fleet of boats nestling in the wake of the Russian cruiser, the faces on deck. During the crossing of the Indian Ocean, he went ashore less frequently with his companions, because of a violent renewal of the fever.

For days and nights, he was troubled with the fear of having to return home, of not being able to finish the journey with his brother, his cousin and their friends, while they continued through the East. From his cabin he could hear their voices retelling each other their adventures with the Egyptian "beauties," in a way that was so different from his own way of telling it, if he could have found anyone to whom to tell it. He was pained to see the interest of his companions in him and his illness wane after a few days— how easy it was for them to accept his absence, to forgo his company. As the days passed, some no longer even came by to say hello to him, but the doctor was forever in attendance, the old bore whom his father had charged to be near him from the very onset of the illness; they said he had always and only looked after patients with this complaint. Silent and dismal, the man was at times as uncomfortable as the fever. Finally, George asked Nicholas to order the doctor to attend him only for the required visits. The next day his brother came in early as usual and found him in bed, already reading.

"I hope you slept well last night."

"As on all other nights, thank you." The querulous tone seemed to Nicholas to be merely the result of an all-too-natural envy.

"We are bored too, we don't know how to kill time. Luckily we get to Bombay the day after tomorrow. I've told the doctor to limit himself to the necessary visits, two a day. All right?"

"Yes, thank you very much. But will I have to go home before you? Tell me the truth ... what does the doctor say?"

"It's not clear, it could merely be an episode that will pass. Don't worry, George. What are you reading?" and with his left hand he leafed through one of the books piled on the bedside table next to the glass of arabate water. It seemed as if no one had looked at them, they lay there still so new, as tidy as the identical days of their reader. More and more, Nicholas's brother remained in bed, only rarely staying up all day. One could hardly tell how tall he was, he'd become so lanky and thin. Why that sickness, of all illnesses, and why his brother?

"Don't change the subject," George said. "Are you sure he hasn't sent Father a telegram?"

"No. In any case, if you want me to, I'll be the one to do so if it's needed," and Nicholas squeezed the cold sweaty hand of his brother; he had never felt it so icy and wet, and was frightened thinking of his responsibility for that life so dear to him. He could feel George's eyes on him, searching to see how long Nicholas would be able to lie to him.

"Can't you see I don't want to go back before everyone? I don't want to go back to Livadia. Can't you see that?" George had lifted himself on his elbow, his hair in disarray, the shirt of his pajamas badly crumpled, the sheets already unclean. Nicholas stood still, resisting the impulse to run away in order not to have to understand that his brother was really wasting away, and that those sheets soiled with potions and medicines were as strong and as sad as prison bars.

"Get dressed, George, get dressed and stop it—you're not ill, you're well, well, well, do you understand? You're my brother, you're not ill, you must not be ill, you mustn't believe it, you mustn't let yourself go. You must get up, go up on deck, play baccarat with us, do you understand? There, take your clothes, take this shirt, the socks, the trousers—there, these ones. Are these all right?"

And Nicholas furiously began to open and slam shut drawers, picking the clothes that should—that must—help George to get back on his feet, that would help him to pretend that he was one of them, a handsome prince on a pleasure cruise. Like a wild creature, Nicholas threw around the cabin clothes that he had seen George wear so many times.

"You've got to stop burying yourself in here every day as if you were really ill, do you understand? You've given in to the illness, you've got to fight it, fight it, fight it, I tell you fight it, damn you!" The cabin was turned upside down; water spilled with the books thrown on the floor, with the jackets, uniforms, coats, socks, unpaired shoes. It was not easy to reassemble George, who, in silence, leaned against the pillows staring at him while Nicholas persisted in rummaging through the wardrobe and yelling in rising excitement. With a slow movement of his right hand George brushed back his hair, buttoned his pajama top and straightened the sheet. He had never loved Nicholas as he loved him at the moment, and never been more keenly aware that there was no escape. The trembling of his brother's voice reminded him of his mother's piercing look from the dock when they left. It was he who had to offer his brother comfort now, give him the strength to cultivate illusions, lie to calm him down. Should he get up to please Nicholas or tell him the truth: that he really could not without feeling his breath fail him? The Tsarevich had just taken out the jacket of his uniform as officer of the Imperial Navy, an identical jacket to the one Nicholas was wearing: he would have to get up; he had to go on deck with the others.

When, that evening, George reached his cabin, taken back by his companions, the first face he saw was his brother's: the thin blond beard, the reddish mustache, the gray-green eyes, the white navy jacket. His own jacket lay in the armchair like a starving animal. Nicholas understood his look, grabbed the jacket, threw it violently to the bottom of the wardrobe. George caught sight of the desolate sword leaning in a corner, the sword he would never use to lead a charge, and the shoes, separated and scattered. There was no possible defense against ruin. He turned to the bedside table where the books were again in order and the doctor was counting drops of medicine into a glass; he saw the jade dancer and smiled. The journey had at least led as far as her, and it was perhaps to the illness itself that he owed his meeting with her. But she was his now; not even Nicholas had gained so much from the trip.

In Bombay the Russian consul brought to the Tsarevich—who had telegraphed the Tsar about George's latest crisis—an order to put the younger brother on board another Russian cruiser. Under the eye of his faithful adjutant, Prince Ourousov, he was to return to Livadia, to the climate that best suited his state of health.

That morning in Livadia, George thought of his father's death four years after the fateful cruise; of the few sovereigns left in the world in that last fragment of the quarter century; of his disease, such a symptom of the general malaise throughout the European kingdoms. In the newspapers that reached even that remote corner of Russia, he saw the daily spectacle of pale princesses of ancient lineage handing over their pale sickly crowns to the new king, money. Populations crushed ancestral crowns under the weight of gold, transformed obedience into a new slavery. But Helen was not of this world; she seemed old in her fealty. Later, after a solitary lunch in a wing of the castle, he took pen and paper to write to her.

The date he put at the head of the letter, January 1, 1900, was a date of defiance against a century in the throes of death. The desk diary on his table was open at the real date, January 1, 1899.

3

WRITING to Helen, George thought of her un-predictability and remembered the day during the last years of his father's reign when they had gone as a family to venerate the sacred image of the Virgin of Vladimir at a monastery close to Moscow; it had been one of the most painful days of his life.

He saw again the long train of carriages with their coats of arms, moving slowly into the courtyard of the convent, welcomed by those nuns who had dispensation from the strict enclosure, the rule that could be suspended only on two occasions—for the visits of the Patriarch of Moscow and visits by the Tsar and his family.

"She really is Aunt Maria Pavlova's sister—look, she has the same black eyes as Helen."

George, wrapped in furs and curled up against the cold at the very back of the carriage with his sisters, barely heard Xenia's murmur as the valet opened the carriage door.

He remembered the fog of that morning, the vision of white figures clustered around the abbess, a princess of Greek origin and aunt to Helen. The Patriarch of Moscow, accompanied by the most senior prelates, went ahead of the Tsar and the Tsarina. The abbess, following the ancient rite, kissed the Tsar's ring and handed him the holy myron, the chrism of oil, balsam and wine simmered with forty-five different species of precious plants, with which the Emperor would bless the waters of the Neva on the day of the Epiphany, as he had always done. The Tsar was anointed by the Lord, and his visit to the monastery rekindled every year the blessings of the Emperor on its occupants, and the more abundant and lasting blessings of God on Holy Russia.

That day the nuns who had remained in their cells heard renewed the treaty of alliance between the sovereign placed by God on the Russian throne and those mirrors of God to the world, the enclosed monks and nuns. The abbess, related to the Romanovs through the marriage of her sister, had withdrawn to the convent in one of the first years of Alexander III's reign. She welcomed the Imperial family with a painful anxiety born anew at each visit; she was almost surprised that these favored beings were not already angels, transformed by the power of the nuns' prayers, those distant echoes from a world submerged in silence. She and her sisters were there to guard and nourish the silence, that it in turn might feed the whole of Russia, starting with the noble princes, as if God could only reach the people of Russia through the Imperial blood. It was, after all, necessary that someone should go ahead into that world where everyone would one day live free of time, and it was the duty of monks and nuns to precede them, to help the Tsar in his task of leading the people to it.

There was a painting in the large chapel of the monastery that showed Leo, Bishop of Rome, halting the Huns by the sheer force of his presence. If only the Tsar could make himself terrible like that saint, could abstain from any earthly vocation to power, peace in Russia would last so long the years would cease to be counted. The Huns were Russia's ancestors; they had been the ones to destroy the Roman Empire. To redress the balance visible only to those blinded by God, it was the Romanovs' duty to refashion the Eternal Empire. For the abbess, who belonged to that dynasty, the justification for the "Highness" in the Imperial title was given by the constant exercise of the eyes in remaining fixed only on higher things. Even naked, even in chains, Royalty had to be seen at one glance as the defenseless Leo had been seen by the King of the Huns: this was the task of the Romanovs. For the abbess, the Russian aristocracy deserved its title only by virtue of the example it set; she knew "Excellence" had to shine forth and dazzle the people, that they be edified, just as mosaics, statues and icons had helped them through the centuries to learn to love God.

That morning she had helped her sisters in the kitchen to prepare the traditional sweets they offered the Imperial family. She felt as if days and years slid away with the signs of erased chalk on the blackboard in the kitchen. The nothingness of slate seemed crowded with features and names, an intricate, inextricable tangle of days, like roots in an overgrown forest. Why count hours, months, years? The visit of Alexander III was the same as that of his father, grandfather and great-grandfather; and already the

Tsarevich Nicholas's cheeks were darkening with hair. It was a mistake to believe in time and death.

"The Imperial Highnesses are no longer children." The abbess looked at George's two sisters with a gentle smile as she ushered the Imperial family into the private study after the church ceremony.

"Your Excellence will remember Xenia's baptism here almost fifteen years ago," Tsarina Maria Feoderovna answered, lightly pushing forward her little Olga, who had hung back shyly.

"A great day for the monastery, I remember it clearly: it was winter and my sister brought little Helen with her. Is Your Majesty aware of Helen's intentions?"

"We know nothing, most Excellent Mother, and are curious, as we are interested in everything that concerns a girl so dear to us." The Tsar had spoken after he noticed George grow pale.

"My niece intends to withdraw here and take the veil."

"We congratulate Your Excellence . . . is it definite?" the Tsarina asked with a shadow of doubt in her strong voice.

"At the moment it is only a wish, but my sister and I are hoping it will grow stronger and take root. I pray the Lord and Our Lady to enlighten her young soul. Everything is so confused in the mind of man, not even silence can help to clarify what the divine will might be. More and more incredible news regarding Holy Russia reaches us, Imperial Majesty: conspiracies, outrages, attacks, attempts on your life, violence of every kind . . . we don't know what to think, we have not yet recovered from our shock at the sacrilege against the person of Your Majesty's father, and already further horrifying news reaches us. What is happening in the world, Imperial Majesty?"

As soon as the abbess introduced these considerations, Alexander III had turned and looked at his absorbed and pale son. He felt pity for both young people, aware of the sympathy that had bound the two since childhood; pity for youth destined to endure and suffer, whether alone or together, whether in the world or in the convent. For a long second he lived again the attempt on his father's life, saw the mask of blood on his father's face and the shredded jacket of his uniform, the stump of leg the adjutant had picked up in a vain attempt to recompose the body of the Tsar from the larger fragments left intact.

"Your Excellence must pray for us," he said, "that God will hear the prayer of the Tsar, sanctified on your lips by silence and renunciation. Holy Mother Russia is indeed tormented by wounds more terrible than those endured even by my father. Yes, Excellence, what you say is true."

The Tsarina was surprised by her husband's tone in front of the children, who were so little used to hearing their father discuss the problems of state that affected him. She looked at him and saw on the strong beloved face the ghost of another whom she had loved as a girl, when she was about Xenia and Helen's age: the Tsarevich Nicholas, her husband's older brother, who had died at barely twenty. Something in the eyes carried the same melancholy.

The abbess shut her lips and lowered her eyes, hearing the wind that at night, after stirring the tops of trees in the cloister, moved beyond to faraway places. Lying in the darkness, she would recognize in the tossing of leaves and branches such a strong, anguished echo of the motherhood she had denied herself that she could not refrain from getting up as if to go to someone's help.

Now, however, she remained still, in silence after listening to the Tsar. Those living icons towards whom all Russians gazed every morning, as they gazed at images of saints high above the votive candles, were there to declare the distance that separates the dead from the living. What then was happening in the world, where so many took up arms to kill? Who was there who believed still in a life apart from death? Was heresy so widespread? Were there really those who committed actions as if they were never to die, as if there were only one way to be, as if there were only the life of the senses, of forms, of the body?

George well remembered the great silence that fell on the room after his father had stopped talking; for him the idea that his Helen should withdraw to a convent had made the sight of the abbess so terrible that he could only stare at her.

The intention turned out not to be true: Helen did not want to enter the convent; it had been a whim, something she had said to see the effect on her family and especially on him. George, however, never forgot the monastery, the abbess, and the study where the first threat to his happiness had been made: he could still see it all before him while he wrote to Helen.

He finished the letter late at night and prepared himself for bed; sleep would be long in coming, and in any case sleep was like a long and arduous field to cross, or like a house full of terraces and steps without railings, with doors open wide to sheer drops, or like precipices of the Caucasus Mountains where he had been as a child. Such was sleep,

open to all currents, swept by every wind and as full of
burblings as a well just before the onset of an earthquake.
He sweated, sharing the effort of the windows to sustain
images of birds in flight around a manor house tall enough
to reach the clouds. He was outside looking in, but also
inside, behind the windows, and if they called him, he did
not know whom to answer, because the voices were numberless and he did not know where he was. Half drowning
in the aquarium that was his mother's palace, he saw himself
walking still and responding to the well-wishing of the
diplomatic corps. The ships that would bring him to shore
moved toward him with painful slowness; he felt he could
not possibly make it and acquiesced as if he deserved all
the water that seeped into every part of his body.

He could sleep only with Helen. He had never been
able to fall asleep if there was anyone in the room with
him, but with her the house of sleep became furnished with
curtains, the light no longer pierced the eyes, the stairs
went down easily and safely, the French windows, free of
any image they had to sustain, simply opened onto a calm
sea. Finally she had arrived; her hands on his forehead woke
him, and she told him how he had talked in his sleep, how
he had called a number of times for his grandfather, Charles
IX, King of France, and for his cousin, the other Charles,
Emperor of Austria; she told him how he had wept at the
treason of the most faithful noblemen after the defeat of
the White Mountain; at the sight of the most treacherous
of all, Waldstein, he had shouted that he be cast out of his
sight, that he never be seen again.

"My love, what an effort History is for you, you seem
to be bearing the whole burden of it. . . ." Blissfully he

received from her hands all the dominions, all the lands, all the names, like the endless titles of the Tsar.

He had wanted so much to dream of her this night, and perhaps he had written such a long letter to induce and help his wish for a dream. But sleep would not come. Long hours had slid by since the servants had put out the lights. He had heard the quarters, the halfs, the whole hours sound from the great clock of the castle. He could not give orders to silence the bells; they were used for the changing of the guards, for the night shift, the day shift of servants in attendance twenty-four hours a day. He lit the light and got out of bed.

There was nothing to do at this hour; one could only exist, and it was a much harder task than any undertaken by the guards who, all around the castle walls, watched over the sleep of one who was wakeful. The soldiers watched, thinking always of the homes to which they would return, homes that awaited them at the end of their long turns of duty. But he himself was at home, yet he too watched.

Suddenly he tore off his pajamas, dressed quickly in the uniform of his regiment, took the cape and sword and left the room, half running. The servant on duty outside his room snored in his chair with his head thrown back and his mouth wide open. Still half running, George crossed a fugue of rooms until he reached the last, where two hussars were on duty. They stood to attention, he answered their salute and raced down the service stairs in order not to alarm the guards by using the main stairway. He knew the password, handed over in a sealed envelope with the medicines: "Resist until tomorrow." Curious. Yes, it was exactly right for him and his guards, he thought, striding toward the walls of the castle. But the news that the Grand Duke was awake and wandering the grounds close to the walls had already been given to the officer on duty by a soldier who, busy among the trees with the daughter of one of the coachmen, had seen him from his hiding place.

"Who goes there? Halt or I'll shoot."

"I'm the Grand Duke, don't you recognize me, soldier?"

"Who goes there? Halt or I'll shoot . . . " but the voice of the guard faltered: he had recognized him.

"Halt! The—the password or I'll shoot."

"Good, good, of course, the password, of course . . . and if I'd forgotten it, if I could no longer remember it? Would you kill me? Tell me, would you kill the brother of the Tsar?" And George burst out laughing, drying his sweat-drenched brow with a handkerchief. By God! Finally something was happening in the house of boredom, he had found a way not to think of Helen for a moment.

An officer appeared. "Imperial Majesty! I'm the officer on duty, Lieutenant Artipov, at your service. What's the matter? Did the soldier show disrespect?"

What business is it of yours, why did you come, why don't you leave me alone? George thought, looking in the uncertain light at the man who was making him aware again of the striking of the hour: four o'clock.

"Go away, Officer, Lieutenant, and tomorrow remember to praise this good soldier publicly. Leave us alone; to resist until tomorrow is not easy, but I'll do it," and the Grand Duke smiled at the soldier while the officer withdrew. He could hear the marching of the guard drawing near for the change of watch.

"Are you still afraid, soldier?"

"No, sir, I'm sorry for—"

"What, what, sorry? You were right, don't make me sorry for the public honor I'm offering you tomorrow. You were right, you would have had to kill me if I'd not at least known 'Resist until tomorrow.' . . . What's your name?"

"Jonas Vyborg, sir."

"Are you Jewish?"

"I, really, I, yes I suppose . . ." The soldier was confused by the question that all his life had been addressed to him, whether spoken or unspoken.

"And why are you frightened? You're Jewish, I'm Grand Duke, isn't it the same thing? There, take a cigarette, let's have one together; you shouldn't because you're on duty, I should not because I'm ill—don't pretend you don't know, everyone is aware they are standing guard over a sick man, you know too. So what! For both of us the end is coming. I've only a little time left . . . and you, I can hear your companions coming to take over." George had meanwhile lit two extra-fine Egyptian cigarettes.

"Thank you, sir, it's delicious. Let's hope the lieutenant doesn't see me."

"But I'm an officer too, you know. Don't you see? Did you think I was merely Grand Duke?"

"I didn't mean to . . . I'll put it out immediately."

"Don't be an idiot, I'm joking. Smoke it, tell me about yourself. Where do you come from? When does your turn of service finish? Do you have a sweetheart at home?"

"I come from Siberia, sir, from Vakytin, a village on the Tobol. I used to work on the river with my father. I'll go back in the spring, sir, when the ice breaks and the fishing starts. As for sweethearts, sir, no, I don't have a sweetheart." The faint flicker from the lamp lit up the pale face of the soldier. He was extremely young.

"I don't have one either."

"Sir, actually there is a girl in the village I like, only I'm not sure she'd like to—"

"Marry you? Certainly she'd like to, Jonas. However, you are Jewish, perhaps she's afraid."

"That's right, my mother always says, 'Remember you can only find a Jewish woman. The others don't want a Jew for a husband,' and it's true. How did you guess?"

"Because I'm Grand Duke, don't you see? Here's your replacement—goodbye, Jonas, you'll see, you'll find the Jewish woman for you in the village."

"Your Highness has some complaint about the guard?"

"No, my dear Sergeant, all's well, there is nothing new of course. . . . Is the password still valid? It's dawn; isn't it tomorrow now?"

"The password has just expired, Highness."

"Well, good luck on your watch. Let's let the good soldier sleep, he must be tired of watching over me."

The Grand Duke had seen the other guardians of his life, Prince Ourousov and the doctor, appear in the doorway of the castle. It was better to go back, to pretend to have chosen to return, not to have to discuss it with them. It was a gray dawn, barely different from morning, from afternoon, from sunset. The windows were not dirty, it was really gray outside. Livadia was no longer the most beautiful place in the world. Sometimes he felt that the magnificent Livadian sun, for the sake of which his parents and the doctors had chosen that area for him, was only an ancient illusion that had to be upheld out of pride and dignity, in case it became clear that the sun shone everywhere with the same power. His brother Michael must certainly have been drunk to have said to him, the last time they spoke on the telephone, that he, George, was the happiest of them without knowing it. Michael only talked when he was drunk, and although it was almost always of himself, he talked in a way that made George wish to stay and listen.

Two years had passed since they had last seen each other; Nicholas had two daughters himself, and had to make up his mind to arrange the transfer of rights of succession to Michael. He, George, ill as he was, would never inherit the throne. Livadia was decidedly not what it used to be, though it was difficult to admit. It was colder.

The two faithful men drew near but he didn't see them; he had turned his gaze to the ships anchored in the roads, to the yacht on which he had played as a child with his siblings, hide-and-seek in the hatchway, behind the long boats, under the awnings, among the thick cordage of long ropes that uncoiled endlessly in the water when they reached a Mediterranean port and dropped anchor. Ah, to be able to live again the morning of arrival at Livadia from the sea, when the full complement of servants and personnel from the castle lined the quay. Such simple and happy people. So unlike the mummified inhabitants of Tsarskoe Selo, like the two bowing to him at this moment. The only difference was that mummies don't talk, and these two never stopped.

"All right, all right, Doctor, I give in, not one word more." Ourousov wanted to add something, but the expression on George's face convinced him to keep quiet, and all three were silent as they climbed the large main staircase between motionless hussars.

"A hot bath, boiling hot, Ourousov, quickly."

Walking through the rooms he had first crossed on the run, he tried stopping at every window to see if anything had changed in the ashen view. But the dawn he craved never came. When he reached the antechamber, he saw the servant rushing to get his bath ready, and grabbed him by the arm.

"You were snoring last night. If I suffer, you too have to suffer. Get out of here. Ourousov, send this idle man to another estate, at my mother's, my brother's, to my sister or to my uncle, to hell, but get rid of him. You know what? He dared to sleep while I was awake! By the way, what were you doing at four o'clock?"

"At four, Highness? I, I was asleep."

"What, you too? You say you love me, you say you live to watch over me, that you will never abandon my service, not even for your young son, and then you fall asleep while I'm awake? Don't make that face, Prince, I too read your letters; did you not think I would? And now I give you full permission to write to my brother the Tsar that I have an intractable temper, that I am neurasthenic, and you only bear with me out of devotion to the Imperial family. Go, go and write and only come if I call you. Good day, Prince."

"Good day, Highness."

He went into the bathroom; the tub was already full and steaming. He stripped slowly, looking at himself in the steamed-over mirror of the antechamber, where he kept the precious Egyptian jade statuette. His body, his sick companion, stared back at him, excessively thin and white. Had it not been for the illness of this body, this stranger, he would have been with her at this moment; there would have been no obstacle to their union. If only he could relinquish to the image in the mirror the illness that wasted his body, that object of such weight and dimensions. . . .

Perhaps there was someone in his brother's great Empire who would break the spell of the mirror, someone who could help him carry into it the fever, the terror of the wait, the seeds of insomnia, the smell of death that had seeped into him and could not be removed, not even from his clothes. . . . He was naked, and his reflection stared at him as if begging him to do something, stared at him until he could see the manacles that held the tortured image of the person he was for those for whom he cared nothing, and who cared less for him. Was there a way, a passage through which to save himself? Through the years, reflections in mirrors had taken from him the certainty that he would make it, stealing little by little everything that appeared of his body; it was mere illusion, a fiction, that he was still whole on this side of the mirror, on the side of the genuinely transient. There was scarcely anything left of himself after so much contemplation in mirrors; but by now more than half his flesh had been secretly saved, in silence, without a word to doctors and popes, saved by a withdrawal from the will to live as others intended. The mirrors demonstrated an allegiance to every possible form; the mirrors received his proposals and pushed them through, beyond him, to a country eyes could not reach, a region hidden to the body, a territory that he would never see, for all that he might strive to turn suddenly and catch sight of it.

In that country lived those gods, the mirrors: they presided over truths that escaped him; they calculated his strength; they watched over the progress of his loyalty to other forms, the willingness given by the illness to trust those different forms. And by now the mirrors were begging him not to turn again, not to ask for further confirmation of the metamorphosis; did he still need to know that someone would look after him, look after his hair, hands, eyes? Helen would like him always, yes, always she would like him, even after the transformations of his body; he felt sure she would. He began to cough. The water was getting colder. He stepped into the bath and lay there a long time with his eyes shut. He opened them only to read the telegram brought to him. it was from Tsarskoe Selo, not from where he hoped: it announced a visit of the Empress Mother.

4

THE JOURNEY had not been tiring. The decision to follow his mother's advice and withdraw to a climate more suitable to his sick lungs, to Abas-Tuman, up in the Caucasus Mountains in Georgia, had given him a little hope. Livadia was again Livadia, its beaches the beaches of childhood summers, its gardens the gardens of delight that they had not been since Livadia had been demeaned to habitual home.

Only once in the two years he had spent there had Livadia briefly regained its delight for him and given him hope. It had been on the occasion of Helen's single visit, with Uncle Sergei and Aunt Elizabeth. Shortly before they left he showed Helen a portrait.

"But it's you, George."

"It's me thirty-five years ago, during an official engagement in Copenhagen."

"What are you saying? The resemblance is extraordinary; who is it?"

"A brother of my father's, the one who should have succeeded to the throne and married my mother, don't you remember the story? Surely you've heard it from your parents? He was the Tsarevich, Tsarevich Nicholas. And he died at twenty-two, leaving his bride to my father. Look, we are as like as two drops, even though I'm five years older than him by now."

He took the portrait to the window. The same blond hair, the same green eyes, the same line for the thin lips, the same threatened, indifferent look, the look of one resigned to danger. And yet there was a shadow in those eyes, a cat could have the same expression of disaffected meekness.

"No, George, you look different, you are you, don't you understand? Stop piling up excuses not to live your own life, stop adding to the things that make you want to give up on it; you must write it yourself, there is no one before you or after you who can do it. Stop searching so hard for yourself in someone else."

"But do you want to write it with me?"

"Of course. But you know all too well who we are."

"See? You too are divided, you too are two people."

"As for that, we are legion, not two," and she had given him a long kiss that had made him drop the portrait. He had hated his body for spying on him like a stranger, an invader who had looked down on them kissing from the ceiling where it had flown as soon as their lips touched; the same thing happened to him sometimes in sleep, when in a dream he felt as if he no longer knew whether he was observed or observer. That day she had reproached him for only being able to look back.

"Who are you looking for in History, eh? Why ransack your family's past? You are unique, unrepeatable, that's why I love you. How could I love someone who will not love himself but looks to someone else, looks to live another's life, escape his own?"

"But if you want me to be myself, don't go away today, don't leave me. Why call my illness 'History'?"

"Because I don't make it more difficult for you to touch me, speak to me, take me, by hiding behind some ancestor or in my family's past. I'm here, I accept to be, simply Helen, and be within myself. That's why I found you, why I could meet you. If I don't marry you, it's because I'm not yet free to do as I wish with myself. But I will one day."

He remembered he had immediately wanted to ask her when, but a clutch of terror had prevented him from asking, had stopped him from speaking, and History had won again in that silence. He had been plunged once again into the endless wait that for others became the past, there where there was room for so many lives, all so contradictory as to cancel each other out. Helen had not come from any past: she was there before him, in this century, without future. She did not want to play with his life as if it were the toy clown whose weight at the base obliges it, whenever it topples over, to straighten itself into the inevitable upright position.

One indistinct part of him was not even conscious of being George, of being a man, of walking on two legs. Yet that was what he was, who he was: George, brother to the

Tsar. And he could move precisely, thanks to that ambiguity. It was true, every once in a while it frightened him, and then he felt the natural terror of losing shape, of losing the memory of his face, the consciousness of being by having arms, hands, legs and of not being able to combine the organic and functional structures of his body with the intangible rest. And yet he loved Helen because she kept him here, in this life defined by his role and the times, defined in a body afflicted by sick lungs; because she refused to let him be engulfed, she threw herself at him to prevent him from leaving, to distract him from his other wish; yet she had no illusion, she knew one day he would break loose from her.

On one extraordinary occasion, in Moscow, she had witnessed him behaving in a way that had revealed the full extent of this aspect of his personality. There had been a brief earthquake powerful enough to arouse terror. She sought him out immediately in the hall of the palace where they were gathered with a throng of people, and found him apart, seated, staring at the swaying crystals of the chandelier with a stunned smile. She knew he was suffering a bewilderment different from the sheer terror endured by everyone else in the hall.

"Come on, George, let's get out of here; what are you waiting for?"

"I'm waiting for the next convulsion, Helen."

"Are you insane? Let's get out."

"Helen, never can we see our faces! They're ours and yet we'll never be able to really see them. . . . It's as if we've never existed for our faces, because we've never even known if we have seen them, we cannot ever trust mirrors."

Swallowing her tears, she had forced him out of the chair, pulled him to a big window. There was no one left in the hall.

"Here is your face, George. Look at it," she had said, facing him and bringing her face close to his, as if drawing his face to a mirror.

George was not sure afterward if terror was the word to define the illumination of that moment, but he was sure that what should have happened to him earlier, during the trembling of the earth, happened now after her words. She was giving him a sense of things that everyone else seemed already to have so abundantly as to be able to waste it. Now he felt like everyone else, and felt it more because he was blissfully conscious of feeling like everyone else; he would have liked to have two mouths, one with which to shout that he was terrified and the other that it was marvelous, that everyone must glory in that panic because it meant seeing before them Helen's face, and that was purest joy. Perhaps woman was nothing more than this, the projection of a terror of man, such a profound and ancient terror that man forgot it in the lavishness of anguish, in the endlessness of terror's courtyards, halls, in its constant ability to assimilate to itself more terror—like Russia, the land able to absorb in its expanse new invaders, new armies laden with gold, without ever losing a blade of grass, without ever losing her identity. And for the first time he was proud of being part of that woman, of that land, of that terror; and proud that he was a member of the family that had reigned over it for three hundred years.

Now, in his new residence in Georgia, in the Caucasus, he remembered that he had not given orders to prepare for her arrival, he had not made ready for her: a room full of light, of flowers, with a fire lit in the hearth. They had passed whole evenings in front of a fireplace some years before in Finland, when they had succeeded in escaping the family's supervision and had fled to the home on the fjords so dear to him for its childhood memories. Under the great coat of arms at Lovisa, in the presence of the stationmaster, who wore a cap with the same eagle present in all the stations of the Empire, they had laid down their royal ranks. This lowly figure in his brother's show of power had no idea of the importance of the only two travelers to get off the train from St. Petersburg that morning.

As soon as they reached the villa, after George's warning to the housekeeper not to tell anyone of their presence, Helen, still in her traveling clothes, had rushed to the great fireplace in the armory, where the Tsar had taught young George to look after the hunting guns, and where George liked to return to smell the oil and wood again.

"Let me make up the fire, George, you sit and read and I'll light it," and she moved from the wood store to the armory, piled the larger branches on the smaller ones, then the logs, as if she had always known what ingredients were needed to give strength.

This too she can do, what can she not do? he thought. In a few minutes she had laid the ingle and lit the first match; the fire leapt up, straight, slender, confident. Kneeling by it, she slowly removed her coat and gloves, with her eyes fixed on the flames. He sat in a nearby chair, took her hand and they remained a long time staring into the flames in silence. What was left of that fire? Where did the strength of woods and mountains go to? Was one obliged to be consumed like wood, be destroyed to give warmth and light? He thought of the thousands, of the millions, of trees burned to such ash to make fire; how happy those logs had seemed to be flame, how content with their fate, how joyously alive in their burning! It was so, then: one had to let oneself be destroyed, swept away. But how could he, with another slow dissolution within him, allow the quick, happy disintegration of fire? A body could only be destroyed once; already he felt the first shivers of the usual fever, which she immediately sensed through his hand. Or was the fever, the disease, the last bastion against the terror of letting himself be consumed and lose his shape?

"You and yours cannot afford to lose, you don't know how to lose," she whispered almost inaudibly.

"To lose? What do you mean?"

"You are panic-stricken at the thought of being trampled upon, ravaged, forced to wander where you may without a name. You are petrified of change," Helen continued, as if struck by a sudden revelation. "You think perfection lies in immobility, that change is a sign of imperfection, death, disease, sin. . . . But only God is unchanging, and just think how alone God is, so still, so silent . . . I shudder to think. Sometimes I think God is my son and that he disappeared as a child. It happens that he is called to rule the world and I, an old woman, learn that the king is my son and decide to go and visit him. The journey is so long it seems eternal. When finally I arrive, they let me in but they laugh when they hear me say that I'm the mother of the king, they cast me out. I stand there, close by the walls of the castle; the king will surely come out one day and I'll recognize him, I'll see that my son is God. Finally, one day a

man comes out with a staff and knapsack, alone, like a
pilgrim; he makes straight for me. 'Let's go,' he says, 'the
way is long to return.' 'But, my son, why return?' 'And
you, why did you come looking for me?' Other times I'm
not sure God will behave so, George. I tell myself that if
he is my son he is also yours, and then both of us, ravaged
by age, will set out to look for him. And when we reach
the castle, we'll see him pass into his glory, we will kneel
in front of God, but we will not recognize him, he will not
seem to be like our son, even when he stops the procession
and runs to us, begging us to recognize him."

At this point George got up, ran to the window, opened
it and, with his hands cupped around his mouth, shouted,
"God, Go-o-o-o-d, where are you? We're here!"

She smiled at first, then grew serious and looked at him
without saying anything, just rose and went to close the
window. Was it the fever or a resistance against being taken
that welled up in him? Was he merely being childish or
did he want to remain a child? The practical ineptitude of
many aristocrats was becoming in George a capricious will
not to lose the right of being always forgiven, the right that
every child in the world has. What was it that made him
fear adulthood so?

"Helen, this happiness frightens me, I fear I will lose
it all." He had interrupted her thoughts as if aware of
what she was thinking. "I'm too happy—what's going to
happen?"

"Everything. We are always at risk."

After a walk the following evening they returned to a
cold fireplace, and George watched her manner change, as
if she could not reconcile herself to having let the fire go

out, not to have thought before they went to guard it so that it would still be blazing when they got back. This disquiet made her incapable of organizing the wood, of choosing the drier pieces, of changing the ash, of making sure that paper was put to help the blaze, of not overloading the ingle with logs. She could not do at all what only a couple of days before had taken her a minute to start and finish. He, silently, to be of help, drew near and swiftly adjusted the wood and lit the fire. She looked at him gratefully but without wonder.

"You could do anything. Why don't you want to?" she asked. Now, in the Caucasus Mountains, he wanted to answer her that the apathy was simply consciousness that he could not change the fate that dictated they be separated by three or four countries and as many languages.

He took up his usual life: correspondence with his family, with friends from the regiment where he had served, the care of his coin collection, walks in the mountains instead of by the sea, the usual visits from local authorities and notables, the consultations with vague and devious doctors, always uncertain and mysterious in their pathetic impotence. And the long sluggish periods of solitude in his room, "thinking thoughts," as Helen had once said. How could all those people in the castle remain in order to serve him? He would not have stayed as long as ten minutes if he'd been well. How was it possible to await an end when there was the prospect of so many adventures in the world? But perhaps the frantic activities of those who were well, the journeys, the work, the deadlines, duties, children, passions, were all precautions taken not to think of the only truth, deceptions behind which she hid—no, not Helen, but the other force, she-death. Always, in any case, the winner. To live ready to receive her, without possessions, without passions, made his wait a long regret that he had not loved death as others did, betraying her all his life.

He remembered his father at Tsarskoe Selo when he came to say good night after their nanny had put them to bed: "Good night! Sleep quickly, children, quickly, quickly—don't waste too much time falling asleep."

Because his father had loved death and betrayed her daily with life. For Alexander III his children's sleep was a dull concession to the needs of the body; he remembered him ill, during his last month in Livadia, with an expression of surprise and bewilderment on his face that was only comprehensible to those who had been put to sleep in such a way so many times: "With all the things I've still got to do," he had muttered in the presence of George and his mother on one of the last days of that October as the confessor, Father Yanishev, came into the room. The death of his father, so soon after the tragic end of his grandfather Alexander, had reinforced in George the sense that there was a predetermined way, that everything was set down, word for word in a script, and that even the necessary bend or turn in a life had been set down. Since the illness had got worse, some years before, one of his strongest wishes had been to be initiated into a knowledge that would lead him to the heart of fate, to read the pages of the volume that would release him from the illusion that he was at liberty to create his life. It had happened thus because everything was written, and he would have nothing to reproach himself with—if he could feel free and able to live out his destiny. But the yoke of freedom had to be lifted.

That was why he hated the doctors, symbols of another illusion. George wanted proof of an ancestral disposition, evidence of a cosmic hostility, but also hope that a balance could be struck in another way after life, starting in this life.

Sometimes he had a vision of his existence within an eternal and perfect disposition, a universe that would set him free of illness, of every imperfection, a universe that would allow him to glimpse a thousand expressions for the imperfect and barely recognized energy he had. And George would sink his life into the ocean of existence; hope would arise not that he be healed of illness, but of life. And he would prepare for immersion into that larger existence with a great sense of anticipation, aware of the numberless other possible lives. No one knew how many there could be, but George felt as sure that he had merely forgotten the others, the ones he had already lived, as that he would live countless others. He had understood the need for oblivion; he knew that there was in a present life a constant development toward forgetfulness, that the divine force that came to the surface as a forgetting of a name, an event, should never be disturbed. Perhaps the spell of the mirror had rescued him from the suspicion that he was not himself but myriad others. The mirror killed any previous experience and was a help similar to the help given by his official life to preserve him from the threat to his identity. To belong to a family that mirrored God and the state was proof of the coalition of previous lives into his, as many rivers merge into a great lake. He had perhaps to find the balance between those existences and his own of prince and patient.

One evening he decided to go into the big hall where

he had eaten many years before with his family, before consumption took hold of his body. He had not been there since he arrived from Livadia, but he had thought of it at various times, remembered the long table under which his legs had dangled as a child, sitting next to the eleven-year-old Nicholas and their younger sister Xenia. That time they had been on their way back from a long journey through Georgia where, his parents had told him, the inhabitants considered him "their" prince because of his name. At the table they had laughed and joked about "George's kingdom." Now, years later, how he would have liked to stroll through a small reign that would be all his own, a kingdom in which every inhabitant is known, where nothing happens that would lead anyone to think the world could change, where every event repeats itself, the king can be king and time can be cut out and made into a cloak to wear at all times.

Yes, Georgia was his kingdom, that was why they gave him that name, and that was why, perhaps, he had so easily agreed to go; his mother had been surprised at his docility. But it was a land as full of contradictions as he himself was. Though small, it had the highest peaks in Russia, and whoever was made lord could reign hidden and undisturbed for a long time. He was becoming convinced that amongst those inaccessible peaks he could reign outside the reach of his brother's Empire. He was fascinated by the fact that in Georgia lived the men who lived longest: it was said there were men who were over two hundred years old. They seemed to love the wait as much as he, but he had to learn from them the secret of making it last for centuries. He would have to question them, understand how they measured time, test the flavor of it, weigh up whether it would be worth plotting an uprising to separate it from the Empire's way of measuring time. He could count on his regiment. He would invite old General Oldorv to the castle, gauge his thoughts on the possibility of revolt.

That evening the long black table was laid as if the Grand Duke did not dine alone: the servants set five places, the number he remembered from the table of the colonel at the officer's club. But Ourousov alone sat at one of the places on George's right.

"My dear Prince, what do you think of the long life of the Georgians? Is it legend?"

"Imperial Highness . . . in every legend there is a measure of truth. In the village at least thirty people are said to have gone beyond the hundred-and-fifty-year mark."

"A hundred and fifty? Let's see, let me think . . . Catherine II had not yet married Tsarevich Peter when they were born. Have you seen them? Have you spoken to any of them?"

"I've caught glimpses of one or two, but if Your Imperial Highness would like to meet them, nothing is easier."

George looked out of the tall windows at the lights of the village. Down there someone was still breathing who had drawn the same Russian air as the great Catherine when she was dying, when in Paris Louis XVI was being killed, while Napoleon was invading Europe, making ever deeper forays into his land, and when Alexander I handed over power to Nicholas I some years after Napoleon's death.

Then the man had breathed the same air as his grandfather and father during their reigns, and was today down there, in the village, breathing the same air as himself and his brother the Tsar. What was he waiting for to speak to him? Men such as he must surely know what it was that he had always searched for. He controlled himself, unwilling to show emotion to the Prince, the man who by order of his brother had for years now never lost sight of him. Helen would have run to the village immediately to see these ancient men. But he could not; he had a plan he must not reveal at any cost. After he had gone into the drawing room to receive the officer on duty and the gamekeeper, he took advantage of a moment when Ourousov was next door talking to the doctor, to ask what they knew of the elders in the village.

"Imperial Highness, my grandfather will be one hundred and twenty-eight tomorrow, but I don't think he remembers exactly, it may be more," the gamekeeper answered warmly.

"Really? I would like to meet him, congratulate him. Bring him to the castle, will you? Or would it be better if I went to him—perhaps walking tires him?"

"He walks like a boy, Imperial Highness. It will be a great honor for him."

When Ourousov came back, George hastened to retire for the night. What a simple way of talking of his grandfather's age; it seemed such a normal thing to that man. Irrelevant. How could it be? Yet the gamekeeper seemed no older than forty; how could he have a grandfather of that age? The sum of the generations grew confused in his mind; he spent a long time calculating how old the son and father and grandfather could be, but the ratio of years that he was used to escaped him. He began to fear he would not know what to say to a man of that grand age; after all, he was a survivor. Maybe it was better to go down to Abas-

Tuman, rather than make him come up to the castle. Maybe he would not find himself at ease in these rooms; perhaps it was better to go to his house, question him surrounded by the things amongst which he had lived a life so difficult for a Romanov to imagine. And his son, how old could his son be?

5

THE NEXT morning George waited by the window in his study. He had practically not slept at all, overcome by a new excitement, as if he had discovered a fresh perspective from which to see his life.

Just as he had in the early days of his love for Helen, he felt gratitude toward his fate. Every adventure gave him the anxiety that he might not be able either to come to its end or to express himself fully through it; happiness clashed in him with the feeling of having barely glimpsed it, without being able in any way to stop it, to set its mark on him. The disease gave him an awareness of time that was all the more precious and selfish because it was constantly threatened. He had already been looking at the clock on the table for an hour. It was large, a noisier clock than the one in the bedroom, a clock that allowed him to notice the time without making it obvious he was looking. Ourousov, the servant, the doctor and the officer on duty had come through; everything was arranged for the new day of his brother's reign. George's edginess had not escaped Ou- ousov, but he attributed it to the slightly higher temperature the Grand Duke had registered this morning, according to the doctor's report. He knew the Grand Duke wanted to meet one of the patriarchs of Abas-Tuman: it seemed an innocent and legitimate curiosity.

Finally there was a knock at the door. The gamekeeper came in with a tall old man.

"This is grandfather, Imperial Highness. He does not see well, but his hearing is perfect."

"Thank you, Anatole. Can you leave us? I'll call you later." The gamekeeper and the others left the room.

George and the old man remained alone. George looked at him: tall, burly, with the long dark face of a precious wood-carved idol, the hair long enough to brush the fur collar, he could be any age. From a distance the face seemed still youthful, but when George came near to invite him to sit, he noticed the net of wrinkles in which were caught the eyes.

"Sit down, do, I beg of you. So how old are you today?"

The patriarch did not answer immediately, but looked around. Liking what he saw, he sat still without speaking, turning first to look out of the window, then at the man standing in front of him.

Strange, George thought. He can't see, yet he looks at everything as if he's already been here.

"I'm as old as my son says. He knows."

"Your son? Is he not your grandson?"

"Perhaps. Do you think he's my son or grandson?"

"I don't know. It depends how old you are."

"The sun has passed over the Elbrus so many times, what's the point of counting? Do you count the number of times you eat?"

"You're right, the years cannot interest those who have so many."

George was surprised at the natural dignity and solemnity of the familiar form of address the old man used. He was the first person outside the family to use it. What struck him more than the expression was the voice, and he tried to think of what it reminded him from the moment the old man started to speak.

"But you are as young as water. The Tsar is young if he has a son as young as you."

"My father is dead. My brother is Tsar. He's two years older than me."

"It's bad when the Tsar dies in his youth. Bad for everyone."

"Why?"

"You must harvest when it's time, not too soon. If you do, the land suffers. Are you the Prince who was here as a child, who bears our name?"

"My name is George."

"I've already seen you, then. Why are you here alone, where is your woman?"

"Have they not told you I'm ill? I can only live here now, in the mountains. My woman is far, in Petersburg. They will not allow her to live with me, she could fall ill too."

The old man sat in thoughtful silence. George did not move, not wanting to break the man's absorption.

"I too fell ill once and they separated me from my woman. But she came after me and I recovered. It's not good for you to be alone, your line must continue. Have you thought what would happen if the Tsar and his children died? You must marry and have children, and your children have to marry and have children, until the last forget the first."

"As you forget your grandson?"

Once more the old man did not reply. George was curious, he had too many questions.

"What's your name?"

"They call me Adam."

"It's a Hebrew name, but you're Russian, aren't you?"

"Do you think I'm Russian?" The clear brittle sound of broken china, pebbles in a landslide, made him realize that the old man was laughing at his questions. He was silent, heard again the ticktock of the clock and realized that for a while he had failed to hear it. Adam stopped laughing and grew quiet, his chin lowered on his chest; the young man stood at the window looking down at the valley where the smoke from the chimneys rose high. The light sound of a waterfall underlined the silence until it began to weigh on him. What point was there in questioning? No one can understand the fate of another. He could listen, yes, but not question; he could enjoy the spectacle of another exceptional life, but neither it nor any other life gave him a lead. Adam's life remained as mysterious and impenetrable as his own. Helen was right; what was the point of asking for reasons to his existence?

"You remind me of someone in your family who liked to live in Georgia," old Adam began, speaking to the silent

Grand Duke. "He was the Tsar of the great war against
the French, against the devil that invaded Holy Russia in
summer and fled from it in winter."

"Alexander, my great-grandfather's brother."

"That's the one. He was like you, he often came here.
The room I crossed on my way here, I think that's the one
where I heard him speak."

"You've already been here, then?"

"Yes, I was young, about your age. The Tsar wanted
to talk to the strongest in the village, he was looking for
twenty of them to form a personal guard corps; he said he
wanted to come and live alone, far away from everyone, a
life of prayer. He wanted to leave Russia to his brother
and take Georgia for himself. He was sure there was a
hidden, cut-off valley where death never came.... A man
like you, he was, the Tsar, with a face like the face of
certain saints, all eyes. He never seemed to sleep."

"I too scarcely sleep."

"But the Tsar did not want to sleep, whereas you cannot
.... The Tsar was looking for the valley that death does
not reach; he was sure it was here in the Caucasus Mountains."

"Did you believe him?"

"Then, yes. And I loved the thought that neither the
Tsar nor I would die, would live forever in that valley.
Now, even if it did exist and was down there, in my village,
I would not bother to look for it."

Finally, George understood of what Adam's voice reminded him: the cry of gulls on the beach at Livadia when
they sensed bad weather; and the turtledoves in the park
at Tsarskoe Selo. A voice that could not be called old,

could not be called ageless; it was not human, it was Time itself, flesh and air, like birds.

"And you, Prince George, you too want to look for that valley even though you're young, don't you? You'll feel as if coming here had a purpose."

The old man talked quickly, as if he had already been in the presence of the sick brother of the Tsar, and wanted to teach him the way never to die. His voice carried the echo of a gathering storm. The eyes closed into slits as he told George his story.

"Who are you going with to look for it? Alone you cannot; you might fall and who will help you up again, who will give you water if you are thirsty? You must look for someone strong and faithful who will love you even without clothes, will love you naked like a child. Go, look for another twenty as handsome and strong as I was, but without eyes that see too clearly, that are too large; look for sheer strength. They say the Tsar was stopped, was prevented from going by a brother with eyes that saw what cannot be seen. . . . But others say that he fled to the mountains and was never seen again. Perhaps he found the valley he was seeking."

George remembered the legends about the end of Alexander the Blessed. So much had been said about that mysterious end. Someone had even suggested that the tomb in the Church of SS. Peter and Paul, where all the Tsars and Tsarinas of Russia lay, be opened up: "Not while I rule, and not while there's a Tsar in Russia," Alexander III had retorted. That meant forever, George had thought. But now the idea of checking the grave of his ancestor fascinated him.

"You, now, don't ask the Tsar to have the tomb opened. It would do you no good to disturb his sleep if he's there, or look for him if he's not," the old man said.

"What would be good for me? To stay here? Would you stay here and merely endure the wait? If you're one hundred and thirty, it's because you have not stood around waiting, isn't it?"

"I've had two women, and both died. We slept together every night. I did not realize I was waiting, because at night they undid what I had done alone during the day; and they doubled my span of life. My women could not bear to go on living after me, so they went before me, because without me nothing but death remained to them. When I saw the first one die, I was afraid. But she wanted to teach me not to fear death, and when the next one died, I was braver. Now that it is my turn, I'm not in the least afraid."

It was late. In a little while lunch would be served. George wanted to be alone, to think about what he had heard.

"Will you have lunch with me?" He was moved by the feeling that he himself could now use the familiar form with the old man.

"It's better if I go home, I eat little, I eat alone. Come and visit me. I have vodka, I still make it myself."

"I'll come, I'll come, absolutely. And thank you for your visit, Adam. I'll call Anatole."

"He's the son of my grandson's son," and the face of the old man moved, unsettling the network of lines, closing the eyes. The smile restored the full ambiguity of the situation.

When George opened the door, he saw himself being

watched, studied, spied upon by Ourousov. He was annoyed, and left immediately through the other door. Later, from his bedroom, he ordered that a sum of money be taken to old Adam. He looked for a gift for him, but could find nothing suitable. What needs could the man have? Capes, goblets, jewels, books, horses, delicacies would no longer interest him. He had everything. And certainly what he needed least of all was money; perhaps it would be useful to him simply as an occasion to bestow gifts upon his family. But who was his family? After three or four generations, families became so loose there is no longer any recognition of power in the blood tie. One is again as free as Adam was, eating his meals alone.

What great service to the race was the love of one's children, and what a deception, what an illusion, it was that the love of these children was destined to be forgotten unless they were born into families like his own, that bore the weight of historical institutions, with the weight to be carried of those who had preceded them in name and patronymic, in the same house and bed, in the similarity of face and voice, mannerism and vice. Everything returned to where it had started, and the story was always the same, as in a magic circle: he, like the brother of his great-grandfather, the Georgia of that time, the Georgia of today. There was nothing beyond the perfection of a circle to give an image to that process, always different and always the same. But what else was the circle if not a metaphor for man's impotence?

Adam's voice was coasting into silence: George's youthful curiosity had lit it, and it had found brief shape and warmth in the cry of birds; but not for long.

George took to visiting the village. Only crises in the illness, and a subsequent prohibition by the doctor, were able to space these visits out, to Ourousov's great relief: it saved him from the questioning to which he subjected the inhabitants of Abas-Tuman every time the Grand Duke had been there. Because of course each time George returned, Ourousov made it his business to hasten to the village, pester whomever George had visited with questions. Sometimes George was irritated by the respectful welcome veiled by suspicion that he received. Why on earth whenever he went into the bar did everyone stop talking, gradually lay cards and glasses aside and take to the door?

One market day he went into the little square crowded with people from nearby villages, and sat outside the bar with the two bodyguards and Ourousov. Immediately the silent proprietor came up to them smiling.

"What is your pleasure, Your Highness?"

"Your own red wine. But what's the rush, Petya? You're going already? What's new, tell me."

"New? Apart from your visits, Highness, here nothing new ever happens."

"You don't mean to tell me that all wives are faithful, no one's died, no baby's been born, the thieves are all in prison and at night no cat ever makes love?"

Watching Ourousov out of the corner of his eye, Petya repeated that he had no news; he was sorry, but it was true.

"Then my visits too are not new, they've become a habit," and George dismissed Petya, letting drop the conversation that Ourousov had immediately attempted to start. He rose, trying to follow the animated barter at a nearby stand between a Tatar peddler and an old Georgian over a Turkish rug.

"Is it a flying carpet? If I were you, I'd try it," said George, smiling at the old man, who lowered his head while the Tatar woman smiled sideways, looking beyond the Grand Duke. As if by magic, all the chatter at the nearby stands stopped and slowly the multicolored mass that had been bustling and buying melted from the square. George went through to the area where fish and cheese were sold and the smell was strongest. There too, after a few minutes the same silence fell, the same tense atmosphere.

"Who am I, the devil that you all have to flee like mice? What's happening to all you blessed people?" He was beginning to lose control and rail against these ungrateful subjects. He had become convinced by now that he was in his own kingdom when he was among them, even though he was careful not to tell anyone, apart from Helen in his letters, and Adam in their talks.

He would have understood his subjects only too well had he seen them a few hours later, receiving rubles from Ourousov. "Remember, then, not a word to him, is that clear?"

But George persisted in trying to get to know his Georgians better, even if, in fact, the only real visits were to Adam in his isba by the stream.

Helen, reading his letters, was aware of a change in George since he had left Livadia. She was not sure whether it was an improvement. Repeated expressions like "our kingdom of Georgia," "my brother's devilry," "soon we will be together in my kingdom," "there is a patriarch who will protect us," "now I've understood how to slip through a crack," "not everyone has died," "an ancestor of mine made it," in a context that Helen could tell was an attempt to lead any spying reader astray, made her fearful. Even his writing had changed, had shrunk, as if George really wanted to hide, to become smaller and smaller, to leave one dimension and pass through to another. She must absolutely try to reach him, to circumvent the careful watch of her parents and the special surveillance that the Tsar reserved for all the Romanovs. One final letter decided her, put an end to all her hesitation: in it George returned constantly to the legend of Universal Judgment, the final moment when Good and Evil would be forever declared and distinguished, as he wrote.

There was such a labored expression of the terror of a death beyond actual death that she feared for him. She remembered that this was not a new obsession of his. They had been instructed for the sacraments together as children with other nephews and nieces of the Tsar. Sometimes at Tsarskoe Selo, Father Yanishev let them illustrate a point to their companions. When his turn came, George had wanted to speak of the Universal Judgment and had terrified them.

With a new look on his face, a strange voice thickened by harshness and tension, he had laid the problem before them: "Either one is saved or one is damned, there is no other way. Either one is damned or one is saved . . . we'll know it only at the judgment. God, though, He knows already! You, Nicholas, Xenia, you and even you, Father . . . some of us in this room are already among the damned, others among the blessed. God, He knows."

"But no, no, George! There is no predestination. How many times do I have to tell you it was the mad heretic Luther who talked of predestination?" the priest corrected him immediately, struck by the intensity of the words, and began quickly to explain again the Orthodox theology of free will.

There is something exaggerated and incongruous in this child . . . it must be the Protestant origins of the Tsarina that give him such an obsession. There is no Russian Gothic shadow, but Danish, thought Yanishev, looking attentively at the pale face of the Tsar's second son, who had returned to sit next to his cousin Helen.

Helen did not tell him her worry: her letters to him had been restrained for years now. Perhaps, she thought, she could take advantage of a long trip her parents were planning through Greece and Turkey, with the idea of going as far as Persia, following in the steps of Alexander the Great, who fascinated Helen's mother. It would not be too difficult to devise a way to separate from her parents somewhere in Turkey, not too far away from the Caucasus Mountains, she thought. But to George she simply wrote of her parents' planned trip.

For a while, though, the preparations came to a standstill: first Helen's mother suffered a long, tedious, if not severe indisposition; then sudden military maneuvers required her father's presence next to the Tsar as commander of the artillery; then renewed hostilities flared up between Greece and Turkey over Crete. There seemed to be a conspiracy against the trip. When the parents were finally ready to leave, new irritating complications arose: Helen's luggage, ready for a week, disappeared. Grand Duke Vladimir Al-

exandrovich's spectacles, without which, shortsighted as he
was, he could not take a step, also disappeared; they'd been
left in a locked drawer with a whole gamut of lenses bought
in England that vanished at the same time. And then the
folder disappeared containing all the money for the various
countries, prepared in readiness for the journey by Count
Samsonov, the Grand Duke's field adjutant.

Despite the unsettling series of obstacles, after a fort-
night peace returned to Greece and Turkey; and luggage,
spectacles and money were again ready. But none of the
travelers were serene as they prepared to leave that morning;
they were already anticipating some new difficulty. The
luggage carriage was at the door, ahead of the coach for
the family; behind it was Samsonov's carriage and the carriage for the duchesses' Cypriot maids. Once the coachman
was in his seat, the Grand Duchess did not even have time
to make the sign of the cross and say Godspeed before the
coach moved off at such a pace that it forced even the
phlegmatic Duke to shout out to slow down. But the speed
increased, became downright dangerous. The Duke and
Duchess both leaned out of the window shouting at the
crazed coachman to slow down, to stop the wild race, but
all they could see was a long whip lashing the horses. Helen,
petrified, silent, gripped hard the sides of the seat and
thought of George, of the delays of those weeks and the
wild run that showed no sign of slowing down. Then it
happened: through the window she saw the strangest clouds
and birds. They were flying peacefully through clouds as
white and soft as whipped cream. Swarms of gold bees
accompanied the incredible flight with their gay humming.
Helen's parents, ashen, hugged their daughter, looking out

at a country so different from the ones they had planned
to visit. They began to pray.

A few minutes later the carriage stopped with a great
jangle of bells in front of the white villa of the governor
of California, in Sacramento, seventy-five years later.

II

THE JOURNEY

6

GRAND DUKE George no longer thinks of Cannes, Ourousov reflected.

It seemed that the air in Georgia really was doing the young Grand Duke a great deal of good; even the fever was giving him a rest. But another fever was taking its place; waiting for Helen, from whom he had not heard for some weeks, seemed to acquire more urgent meanings beyond the private nature of his individual threatened life, meanings that were ancient and belonged to no one. Adam continued to offer him homemade vodka in the isba, where gradually the old man's few contemporaries began to gather regularly. Only the children listened to them as wide-eyed as the brother of the Tsar, and only they asked that the story be told again.

"We'll end up dying while we tell the story and never know we've died," Adam had said once, looking at the Grand Duke holding an empty glass. And George's shining eyes seemed to acknowledge the beauty of such a death. Adam's three friends were all roughly as old as he, but they too did not remember their exact age.

Vassili had finally arrived that day. Adam had already spoken of him: "You'll see, Vassili will talk to you, he'll tell you what you want to know. I had him called from his village. They know him too," he had said, pointing to Gavril and Piotr.

As soon as he opened Adam's door, George was met by the strong currents of an animal life. Like a land stampeded by horses, penetrated by fish that caressed its shores, he observed, stunned, the ebb and flow, the surging of dead and living animals and humans, a swirling of writhing flesh. And below the surge and swirl shone Helen's laugh. At Adam's door the life he did not love disappeared and he glimpsed another: Ourousov never came in with him; George had not even had to order him not to.

Ah, to be able to find the link in the chain that united his to that other existence! . . . After a glass of vodka Vassili began to tell of a trip he had made as a young man, under Tsar Alexander, a hundred years before.

"At that time I was servant to a count who in winter took me with him to Moscow. His name was Golovkin. The Tsar, your great-grandfather's brother, had put him in charge of an expedition to China, and I was one of those chosen to go. I can still remember the wagon with the notebooks and notepaper. Before we left, we all had to wash from head to foot with a special soap for protection against the Chinese diseases, different from ours. The Emperor of China had enough diseases without wanting ours as well.

We were on the point of leaving when some horsemen reached us, couriers from the Emperor, to say we were too many; we had to cut back as if we were to pass through a very narrow gate. I, who very much wanted to see China and was well treated by my master, did not want to drop out and did not know what to do to make sure I wasn't. But I was good-looking and the Chinese mandarins liked handsome men, so I was selected. Only the number of servants was reduced; the Tsar refused to reduce the number of the nobility to go with him, and he was right, why should he? We had crossed the whole of Siberia, we were already at the border with China when more emissaries arrived to tell us we must cut down more on the number of men: the Emperor of China considers us his vassals and does not want too many "impure feet" in his Empire. . . . We rebel, but can do nothing. My master, Count Golovkin, goes back and forth between our encampment and the Chinese camp for a month to negotiate. And what is more, our Tsar had sent the Emperor some wonderful gifts. But the Chinese want us to kneel nine times to the Son of the Sky, as they call their Emperor.

"We don't quite know how, but the count succeeds in getting permission to pass, and we enter the country, preceded by the wagon of gifts and the torches of the Emperor of China. One member of the expedition—he had a hooked nose like an eagle—wrote every day on a sheet of paper this big; he showed it to us every once in a while. We could see the rivers, the forests, the cities. He could even draw the animals, the blue foxes, the squirrels, the tigers, the stoats. It was wonderful to walk where he afterwards would make signs, record it in ink. We reached Mongolia. The freeze was such that tea became ice as soon as it was poured.

"One day a long line of tiny horsemen clad in red comes to meet us; they were escorting a closed carriage borne by four men. We thought it was their Emperor, but it turned out to be the Mandarin of Mongolia. Our gifts were beautiful: there was a long golden dress, so long that to wear it eight men had to hold the train; some tall black chairs made of a wood only the Tsar had in his rooms; rings that only the Tsarina can wear, they are so shiny; a narrow long kind of boat that the king of a seaside city had sent to Tsar Peter, who was as curious about boats as the Emperor of China. But that mandarin! He yelled and screamed like a woman, and made himself quite clear: he wanted something that was not amongst the gifts and that we could not give. The count understands that they want the gifts to be a sign of submission to the Emperor on the part of the Tsar. You can imagine us seeing the Tsar's gifts thrown back in our faces. We didn't want them, and threw them outside the encampment. At the border the Chinese caught up with us with the gifts and threw the gold dress, the black chairs, the shiny rings, the slender boat Tsar Peter had liked, over onto our land. Only the man with the hooked nose like an eagle entered China, because he could speak the language. We waited for him at the border for twenty-seven days, and when he reached us he showed us the map of China he had been able to draw by stealth, by cutting the paper into narrow strips and sewing it into an internal pocket of his waistcoat. Count Golovkin didn't want to believe it; it was impossible that the Chinese should leave him free to

draw. But he was unruffled and told him that if he had
invented the map, everyone would be able to use it at a
distance with equal advantage. The man understood more
than many, as others with faces that resemble eagles understand. That night I sought him out in his tent and asked
him to tell me what China was like, the one he had drawn
by stealth, not the other. And he began to tell me.

" 'As soon as I arrived in Peking, they took me in front
of the Son of the Sky.'

" 'But why did they give you permission to enter into
his presence?' I asked him.

" 'Because I alone bowed to the portrait of the Emperor.
There is one Emperor, but he has many faces: here he is
the Tsar, there he is the Son of the Sky, in France he is
Napoleon. To bow to one man is to bow to any of them.'
He said just that, the man of the eagle face, and went on,
'When the Emperor saw me, he wanted to question me
about our people and I told him many things. But he only
wanted to know whether the Tsar was happy, if he too was
looking for something he felt he missed. I told him that
our Tsar was a happy man, he had daughters, a good
Tsarina, faithful subjects, a faithful army, and he answered
that he too had almost all those things. What he wanted
to know was whether the Tsar feared never to wake when
he went to sleep at night. He himself had everything, but
was searching the Empire for the place where he could live
without this fear. Someone had told him that in the land
of the Tsar, amongst white mountains as high as the sky,
there was a valley where one could live so. He begged me
to ask the Tsar to begin looking for this valley that his
magicians saw in Russia, and then send word to him as soon

as it had been discovered. He was ready to hand over all the northern provinces to the Tsar in exchange for what he sought, he had an edict ready to this effect. He gave me a stone as a gift; he removed it from his crown and shook hands with me in a way I've never been able to forget, because the look on his face was so similar to that of my most beloved dog when he was dying. When I left, he accompanied me as far as the walls of the city; he went to the highest guard tower, and I could see him until he vanished in the horizon. To the last he kept hold of my hand, tightening his grip, looking at me fixedly and repeating, "Remember." '

"When the man of the eagle face had finished his tale, he added that he could not fail to keep his promise. He had two maps in mind: one, stolen from the Emperor of China, where the Tsar could read that in his Empire, in the mountains of Georgia, was the valley death cannot reach; and another, stolen in turn from the Tsar to give to the Emperor of China, where he would be able to mark down the valley among the most inaccessible mountain chains of his land. The man knew the Tsar personally; he said he had the same eyes as the Emperor, that all of you have the same eyes. He felt sure that Alexander as much as the Emperor suffered from not being able to sleep, out of a terror of death. He hoped only to live long enough to reach Alexander and return to the others, to free himself of the memory of the expression on the Emperor's face. I think he made it, from what we understood when the Tsar came here about eighty years ago, to ask us to join him in the search for this valley. But he underwent a strange end: after keeping the precious stone given him by the Emperor in his pocket for many years, one day he had it blessed by the Pope, inserted it in the barrel of a gun and blew his brains out."

While Adam rekindled the fire and Gavril went on pulling on his pipe, a big black cat came near and rubbed itself against George's legs.

"The Tsar had the eyes of a cat," muttered Adam; "they slid over people, they knew no one lasted."

George fixed his eyes on the fragment of mirror next to the icon of Mother and Child; in every house mirror and icon were placed side by side. So all the earth must be the valley that did not permit death; there was no other vale but the earth. It was dark; only the fire lit the ancient faces of the patriarchs who had been handsome enough to trouble the sleep of women, strong enough to give credence to the illusion of a Tsar that he could cross the mountains to where there was no death. Perhaps they had outlived women, children, masters. Perhaps they had perceived his coming like that of Alexander the Blessed, had felt in his own arrival the same quality as the coming of the conqueror Napoleon to seek among them an even more terrible enemy to vanquish. And now only the misery of decline, the crumbling of the senses were witness to their superiority. He could only cling to these wasted bodies for a thread of hope. How was it possible that the dream of immortality was testified to most clearly by those closest to death? Why did he think only of the past when he saw them, of years that were no longer? What happened in the home of these old men to blind him so that he saw nothing except the stone of Alexander leaving with his valiant twenty? What was it in him that, faced by the four ancients, started to question the dead, consult the absent, to live dreams, fantasies, fictions? Why did it seem to him that Adam's body multiplied into dozens of bodies, one on top of the other, higher and higher until they had formed lofty towers, each body corresponding to one year in the life of the man and a fraction of the space that formed the dwelling of the Tsar and Tsarina, that pullulated with battles, peace, seasons, famines, plagues, earthquakes, harvests, the children of that year. And if he lifted his eyes to the sides he saw the same things, slightly faded, arranged a little differently, perhaps the horses, bishops, knights, kings and queens on a chessboard. The bodies are the tall towers that span the provinces of time; it seemed to him they were always murmuring "we were there" if he failed to look up as he crossed the square of the village and watched the people. And if it was true, what Adam said, that cats could sense the transient nature of people, perhaps they saw what he saw. Was this why in many regions of the earth cats were held in awe, as if they were divinity?

He looked at himself again in Adam's mirror, in the darkness of the room, and felt that his inability to see in the dark, unlike cats, was a truce, a sign that he could go now. He wanted to write to Helen that very evening. What day was it? But that day, that number, that very hour had been marked in his life twenty-eight times already. They repeated themselves, they repeated themselves that he might forget what was in those days, in that life. There was no way he could remember this day of the previous year or the year before that. Memory only wanted to live underground; on the surface there was mere oblivion.

"Where is your woman?" Adam asked.

"She is traveling, not far from here."

"Are you still ill?"

"Yes, but I'm getting better."

"Then call her to you and don't think of Tsar Alexander anymore. Take your woman to bed with you, not the disease."

George left the isba and the night cold penetrated him to the bones; he keenly felt his flesh, gratefully reawakened by the tenderness of his memory of her. That body still held him back, he was still young. Immediately the two soldiers were at his side to escort him; he looked at the slope that vanished up in the darkness toward the lit castle.

When you come, we will not light the lamps, he thought.

7

"N OW HE'S as sad as he used to be," Ourousov muttered to himself, the faithful servant engaged in constant observation of his master. Through the unfolding of
the months and years of their communal life, it was becoming sometimes difficult to tell which of them was in fact
the master. Ourousov's glances, his letters to the Tsar, his
visits to the village—even his rare absences—more and
more gave the only shape to George's day. In these days
George no longer left the house so frequently to visit Adam
and his companions. Instead he spent the day in an idle-
ness that might seem depression to someone who did not
know George's meditative nature.

For him not to do anything was not sloth. He was sure
he participated in countless events by the simple act of lying
on his bed for hours with his eyes open to the dim light.
He felt his silence nourished events that otherwise could
not take place, helped him to recognize step by step how

these events came about in their nameless anonymity. He was beginning to have a different sense of the wait, as of something that could not be fulfilled. It was possible that the immobility still helped the transparence he sought and that the depths could be seen. These were days when he no longer complained, when he sensed the complete uselessness of action and speech, and when he would feel the warm pulsing of blood through his body as part of the general current in a sea that was life, and he regained the shock of surprise at the constant stemming of the flow of nothingness that made up life. He was not frightened at this, merely in awe at the harmony of his flesh with the air he breathed: he tasted Time in its pure state. The cooperation of such precise and fragile powers made up what he was, and though there was no commitment that the cooperation would continue, still it was him that was the miracle not to be proclaimed from the rooftops. His concentration worried the doctor, who thought of it as a symptom of deterioration of George's condition. George let him increase the dose of drugs without protest, and threw the medicines out of the window at night, smiling and thinking of Adam, whose isba by the river he could see from his room. Yet those men had had to tap some secret power; no one on earth lived that long. What magic lay hidden in his Georgia?

After the enthusiasm of the first days, George had become estranged from his "subjects," as he called them. Perhaps he, his immediate circle, had caused the estrangement. He had never forgotten the speed of the exodus from the marketplace the day he tried to draw close to them, and he had noticed at other times the same care to avoid him. Only Adam's patriarchs had made him welcome. His jailers wanted him alive and made him burn slowly to save on his scanty supply of energy. Helen could light the flame, and George would return to Cannes, to Militza of Montenegro's villa.

Finally one day he gave the order of departure.

"To go where, Imperial Highness?"

"Is my brother's Empire so small that it is impossible to leave, that one can only remain? To leave, I said. Get things ready, if you will, Ourousov. I want a team of men with all we need for an excursion of a few days in the mountains. Don't ask me how many days, don't deprive me of the pleasure of going for the sheer pleasure of going."

The Grand Duke's doctor, on immediate consultation, could find nothing against it: a few days in the mountains would do him good.

They left the castle early one morning and took the permanently snowbound path toward Elbrus, the tallest mountain in the Caucasus. The regal mass rose up against the horizon, behind the trellises of the lower mountain chains; it was the symbol of all that George sought, that toward which his life was directed unknowingly. Because although he could pretend that the sight of it was enough, the mountain had in its vertical arrogance the very boldness of being that George aspired to. The more deeply his contemplative nature plumbed his spirit, the more powerfully he would sense a refusal to become a mere current and merge with the faster currents of a river that, once united, never changed the pace of its unrelenting flow. He questioned the mountains, the waterfalls, the passes, the glaciers: Alexander had passed through there; Adam had told him so many times. It was the route his forefather had taken, from which no one could be sure he had ever returned.

The landscape was grimly beautiful: rocks without trace of life merged into sheer peaks in an expanse that refused to accommodate the travelers. George felt the hostility of the landscape, the denial of the human dimension with its alterations, changes, corrections. A victorious war waged by Catherine II against the proud Georgian people must have been the reason for the annexation of the mountains to the Empire; but Mount Elbrus had not heard about it, the glaciers knew and cared nothing of it.

A certain unease took hold of the men who carried the tents, the food supplies, the arms. By the second day they had stopped singing, not because the paths were narrower, steeper, nor because the pauses were not long enough for them to rest. The Grand Duke bewildered them, frightened them; that air he had, ever graver, more severe, his evident distance from them—he who normally was so friendly and warm—his hurrying onward and his deciding, where an ancient hand had left a directional sign, which route to follow without consulting anyone, not even Prince Ourousov. It seemed as if he already knew the way; sometimes—always ahead of them—he would stop as if he were talking to someone. But to whom? What did the man see in the mountain he was journeying toward with such decisiveness? The food supply would certainly not be enough to reach the foot of the mountain; their equipment was light, suitable only for an excursion. At a bend in the path a black stag appeared, surely the most majestic creature ever seen in those mountains: it made the carriers shiver. Was the brother of the Tsar in fact talking to the animal?

Ourousov seemed the most worried. He tried to catch the Grand Duke's eye whenever he made a move as if to turn. Since George had come across the stag, he felt sure that Alexander had got rid of his porters. They could not have gone through certain gorges; some passes had to be crossed one man at a time. It was now the second evening of the journey. George ordered the men to set up camp and immediately three tents went up, one for the Grand Duke, one for the Prince, one for the men. The stag had vanished.

"Highness, tomorrow we will have enough food for only one day, what is your command?" Ourousov asked, fixing the young Grand Duke with a stare as they dined by the fire.

George had never met the eyes of his guardian for any length of time, and he thought he saw for the first time all the evil that had accumulated in him. An instinctive repugnance prevented him from looking any longer, and he tried to delay the answer; surely Ourousov had not always been so repugnant? Who was this man who sat next to him this evening facing Mount Elbrus?

George almost did not recognize his own voice when he replied, "You didn't mean provisions. You meant something else, you meant reasons to live."

"No, Highness, I didn't mean reasons to live. And last time the provisions were enough."

The bread he was holding dropped from George's hands, and he looked around, trying to get the attention of one of his men. But there was no one around the fire, only the wind beating against the empty tents and setting them flapping. Alexander had remained alone on that same road, alone with him.

"So you know the way," George whispered, looking at the clearing where five men like him had sat and now only the fire breathed.

"You too, Highness, just like Alexander, but without the decisiveness of the stag I sent. You are young, you are only half convinced, unlike the Tsar, who was absolutely certain.

"Helen, why aren't you here, why don't you help me?" George, immobile, saw her again in Finland, at Lovisa, crouching to light the fire.

"She, she is the one who has prevented you from acting resolutely. Tsar Alexander was older; he prepared for this expedition with great style, it was not a three-day excursion like yours. . . . He'd forgotten Elizabeth, he had not loved her for years."

George could feel the evil all around him, as if the sheer peaks, the two-day march stood like a revelation from powers that passed through that region every hundred years.

"Anyway, Princess Helen is far from home; it would be difficult for her to hear you, Highness, for a while. First she has to convince the governor of California that the skyways are also open to me. That's not easy, the governor has little imagination even though he's an ex-actor; he's doubtful, doesn't want to believe either Grand Duke Vladimir or Grand Duchess Maria, or indeed Helen herself, dressed as they are in costumes that are seventy-five years old."

Ourousov whistled and a revolting creature appeared. The gay lifting of a long tail emphasized the inane smile on the pointed face.

"You see, Highness, such were the fish that dwelt in the sea before a yawn of the earth raised these high mountains you so like to contemplate. You will forgive us, I hope, for making it appear for your benefit; they were so homesick for their lord, these creations of mine. . . . Sometimes I'm so sick of keeping close to you in the guise of that Prince; I understand you so well. I don't like him at all, he has no charm, no sense of irony. The company of this creature of mine amuses me, though, and anyway poor Prince Ourousov will suffer a miserable end some years hence, right here in these mountains. I feel sorry for him; it can't be very nice to be buried alive with one's son."

"What do you want from me?"

"From you, Imperial Highness? Really! It's you who have been seeking me for so long, I should be the one to ask the question."

"I want Helen."

A long terrifying laugh came from not one but a hundred Ourousovs. George looked around but could see no other creature.

"You lie; forgive me, Highness, but I have to say it. You cannot lie to me, though you may to Ourousov. You no longer only want Helen—come on, be honest."

"You don't want Helen alone, be honest," croaked a second creature suddenly on the scene, hugging Ourousov's bare legs with its fins and cackling under its big whiskers. Ourousov no longer wore the uniform of a major, nor the cap with the Imperial eagle. A kind of broad-rimmed miter, like a cone with the base at the top, extended itself into the darkness; but half of it was missing to reveal an open skull with the white pulsing mass of brain exposed. George had dared to look. A light went on behind him, then another on his right and another still higher up.

It was morning. He was in his room in Livadia, in front of the sea, during Helen's last visit; she wore a long blue-and-rose crêpe dress that she knew he liked.

"My love, it's me! Wake up, what are you doing? How do you feel this morning? Don't you remember, we're supposed to visit Sevastapol today? You look wonderful. . . ." It was as if a sprite had gagged him and all his efforts to free himself served only to fix the gag more firmly over his mouth: he could not speak. He tried desperately to reach the bell by the bed.

But the light went out and again he could distinguish the outline of the distant Elbrus and the Caucasus range.

"You see, Highness, I don't doubt you want the Princess near you; you want her as well. Some thousands of years ago another Prince just like you kept on insisting as they were chaining him to those rocks that he had stolen fire out of love—out of love of mankind, that is."

George lifted his eyes and saw Ourousov, naked, next to the ogre of the fairy tale that had most frightened him as a child, a horrible creature with an enormous belly and eyebrows as thick and black as a beard.

"Are you surprised at this dear ogre? Do you want to look forward forever, to plan, never to die, like the Prince with the fire whose liver, gnawed by the eagle of these mountains, grew again to be gnawed again incessantly? So I have to show you Leonida, he who will rule your land in seventy years' time, Highness. They will take him from here, the new ruler, from the dwelling place of the childish terrors of a brother to Tsar Nicholas II, the source of his fear of the night. . . . Come on, get up, Leonida, don't stay sitting there, his brother still reigns. Your turn will come, but now you must still bow to His Imperial Highness." And the enormous ogre made a movement that imitated the grace of a bow. Immediately two repulsive attendant creatures rushed like furies to Ourousov's side to support him and reshape him into his spellbound pose.

"Leave me to die in peace." George could not stand the vision and hid his face in his hands.

"Highness, what lack of originality in your request; you disappoint me . . . Prometheus was much more demanding. Your request will be granted without my help, don't you think? You shouldn't have bothered to summon me. Keep your illness and moan to Adam, if that's what you want. . . . Poor Ourousov would be so happy he might even shed a few genuine tears of regret! And if we were to return home? Perhaps there you'll be more convinced as you wait for Princess Helen: you'll look at yourself in the mirror morning and evening, just as the other one did who wanted to pass by here and never die. Will the spell of the mirror break and reveal your face?"

Immediately, George was in his room in Abas-Tuman. On the desk was an open letter in Helen's handwriting, on top of letters from his brother and his mother. There was a knock at the door, Ourousov's knock, two soft taps and one more decisive. George looked at himself in the large baroque mirror with the five lights and saw five Georges leave the mirror in five bodies like his own. He watched the bodies bearing his features walk toward the door and open to Ourousov, whose mild face was as expressionless and dull as it always was.

"I see, I see, I understand, Imperial Highness. I won't disturb you until lunchtime." Ourousov had answered the overlapping murmurs of the five Grand Dukes George Alexandrovich Romanov, who had spoken of him, George Alexandrovich Romanov, with obvious worry. And when all six had left, George saw, trembling, that the mirror reflected nothing; there was no image, and on the ground lay the carved Imperial eagle, torn from the baroque frame, with its wooden wings broken: wood lice had finished their arduous task that very day. He lay on the bed and closed his eyes. God had to help him. God had to send Helen. He had never refused pain, but the horror was too much; he could not bear it, would rather die.

8

My head, it seems, is in a forge
And in the smithy the sound of beating
Up, then down,
Again, again.

The hammer hitting
Echoes, grows in echoing walls
Here and there,
Echo, echo.

And my poor brain, poor little brain
So stunned, no reasoning
can, not can,
Goes mad, yes mad.

[—from *Il Barbiere di Seviglia*]

GEORGE, still clothed, was awakened by a thin voice singing in an unknown tongue, and recognized the voice of Ourousov. Then there was silence. What could he do? It was impossible to tell anyone what had happened, it was the loss of some faculty—like the ogre, the monstrous future ruler of Russia that had emerged from his subconscious. He smoothed out Helen's folded letter, which had already been opened by an indiscreet hand. His own confusion of spirit must have permeated through to her. She wrote of the wearying trip from which she and her parents had just returned, profoundly exhausted in body and soul. She wrote in a different style, less fluent and penetrating, with omissions and delays. In its cautiousness it was as if Helen wanted to tell something else, something she was sure no one would believe. Her repeated insistence that she was about to come to Abas-Tuman was made with an apprehension absent from her other letters.

George answered her with a certain guilt; he recognized his responsibility for the tiring and strange journey of his woman. He felt as if he had not done enough to prevent it, that he had focused too much on ghosts of immortality in the last months, that he had neglected the distant Helen.

Adam had said put the woman, not the illness, in your bed. Instead the illness had taken him by the hand and kept him company every day. He opened the letter from the Tsar, who wrote, after the habitual affectionate expressions of greeting: "Your faithful adjutant is worried at your melancholy, and writes that he would like to distract you with some excursion into the beautiful Caucasus Mountains. The doctor sees such marked improvement that he has also agreed to a cruise that Ourousov will propose to you. We've told him of our approval and since we believe, dear George, that you'll be going around the world, we won't write for a while. Alix is in as good a state of health as her condition permits: God will an heir for our dear Russia. Olga and Tatiana send greetings and many affectionate thoughts," etc. etc.

Around the world with Ourousov? His blood froze. What machinations now? He rose, holding his mother's letter and leaned out of the window. It was a clear, mild day, with no wind, everything was busy, happy to exist, the clouds, the waters of the river, the smoke from the chimneys of the isbas. Why fear? What was different from any other morning? It was the year of Our Lord 1899, the fifth of his brother Nicholas's reign; the Empire was at peace. He looked at the closest houses, following the movements of the inhabitants to and from the market. He spent over an hour at the window watching life being lived, taking note of the actions with which people made time fly to realize at midday that they were hungry. Being at the window restored to him the sense of a time that was not present unless it was felt. He left the window to sit down and read the letter from his mother. She was happy at the news of his improvement; she too knew of the cruise, had been told by Nicholas. She would have wanted to see him, to speak at length on a matter about which surely his brother had written to him: Catholic Poland, the Popish country, the rumors of a Poland separated from the Empire, with Grand Duke George Alexandrovich, brother of the Tsar, as Sovereign. Those wild fantasies had indeed given play to tasty gossip in the drawing rooms of Petersburg but he could relax, no one had really believed the Grand Duke could hold with such absurd ambitions. His loyalty to his brother and fealty to the Empire were too well known. He was not to worry if news to the contrary should reach him; the Tsar had never given credence to such senselessness or thought for a minute that one of his brothers could aspire to reign. And she herself, who after all best knew her George, knew that for him the kingdom of the imagination, where he had reigned since childhood, was enough; only yesterday she had read to little Tatiana one of the fairy tales he had written when he was ten.

George folded the letter slowly. Yes, Mother was right; in the end, Georgia was nothing more than his imagination, his kingdom. And it gave him many worries, many more than Nicholas II's affairs of state. His apprehension went to Ourousov, but he held the thought back, tried to distract himself, answering his mother and brother with letters that were perforce conventional.

At lunch, punctual as on every day, he sat at Ourousov's left. The adjutant revealed nothing, the same deference and discretion present as always in their conversation.

When they reached the fruit course, George took his courage in his hands and confronted him with the subject of the cruise: "His Imperial Majesty informs me that soon we'll go on a cruise."

"I'm very happy, Imperial Highness: it was a proposal of mine and the doctor's to distract you, and always hoping it will benefit your health. His Imperial Majesty has deigned to approve it."

"Your concern is touching. When are we to leave? And where will we be going?"

"What? Has Your Highness not yet read the map of the journey? It's on your desk, it explains the full itinerary. We've tried to conform as much as possible to your wishes, wishes that after so many years at your humble service we could not fail to know. On the other hand, Your Highness will fully understand that because certain wild voices in Petersburg have reached the Tsar, nothing will serve better to silence them than your temporary absence."

Now his voice echoed with the sardonic lilt of the other Ourousov. George finished his fruit and rose. If Helen were to arrive, where would she find him? And that letter from Nicholas never mentioned Poland, but took the cruise for granted—what were the machinations behind this? Did Nicholas really want him to disappear temporarily? Or was the letter written by Ourousov? George withdrew to see what papers were to be found on the table. He could find no map, no details, no itinerary, only a thick empty notebook and a goose quill, the pen Aunt Alexandra, Princess of Wales, had given him as a child. It had belonged to Lord Byron; he remembered the pen well, and the illuminated Bible, gift of Uncle Edward. He sat on the bed and covered his face with his hands.

"Why? You mustn't be sad, it's so wonderful to travel," said a voice. Next to him, sitting on the edge of the bed, with his own blemishes on the back of his hands, his own diamond ring on the ring finger of the left hand, was himself, George. Had one of those who had escaped from the mirror returned?

"Why are you afraid? One always returns home, one never truly leaves."

"And the others, where are they? Is it only you?"

"The others are waiting for you on St. Helena, in Paris, Peking, Rome. I'm here to persuade you to be more honest with Ourousov. See?" And, with the nervous left hand streaked with veins, he pointed to the mirror where one of the lights reflected his dejected image.

"Now let's not waste time if we want to return to the mirrors all together. Write down the journey you would like to take; write the itinerary to send to Helen, although you have no need, you've told her so many times in your dreams." George rose as the other rose; both sat at the desk and while one dictated the other speedily wrote. It was like entering Adam's isba: a current he could not halt carried him with it. Beyond the window the tall peak of the Elbrus looked down.

And as George wrote, everything seemed to become clearer in his mind, as if all he had to do was simply change to the first person singular what had already been written by others in the third. He felt as if he could finally remove the dust from the masks, costumes, the sets of old plays in which no one acted, since actors could no longer be found of the stature of Napoleon, Louis XVI, the Roman Pontiff, a young Emperor of China. He knew everything about them; he had dreamed and imagined them too many times to be able to ignore their secret thoughts, their more subtle moods, the last and definite truth that mirrors reveal when they are freed of their bonds and they hand over to the white page the terrifying talent of reflecting the face of a man. And the white pages under George's hand became filled with words, starting with a day on St. Helena, one January Sunday, 1816.

9

THE principal town of St. Helena is no more than a group of houses running a short way along a narrow valley between two sheer mountains.

I arrived on the island on Sunday, the seventh of January, 1816. As soon as we reached the shore, we were escorted by an English platoon toward Plantation House, the residence of the governor, Sir Hudson Lowe, who had already been informed of my arrival; the whole island was equipped with signal towers, so that if anything at all happened it could immediately be referred to its uneasy governor. When I was shown into his presence in the comfortable neoclassical villa, I felt less like despising than pitying the man. Here was the one picked by fate to be Napoleon's jailer and executioner. His task was to render the life of the great ruler so odious that he might find death more desirable; thus Napoleon would endure forever the antipathy of posterity.

"It is a great honor for us to welcome the nephew of Tsar Alexander on St. Helena," he told me, and bowed with a sudden bobbing of the head forward that seemed an effort to swallow better. I could not hide for long a certain unease while he praised the climate, the healthy air; the mild winds; the good, alkaline, slightly diuretic waters. I interrupted to ask him without more ado how Napoleon was. For a fraction of a second he shut his eyes, as if forced to inhale an intensely unpleasant smell: he had not had time to investigate with what attitude a member of the Imperial family would drop anchor at St. Helena, and had not yet even told the prisoner that I was there. I had spoken too soon and was immediately suspect; I could see it from his half-closed eyes. Hudson Lowe had no way of knowing that I dwelt on an island with a name identical to this one—as does every man who loves or hates and pays a ransom for his freedom.

"General Bonaparte is in very good health. I've never seen a man with a more ravenous appetite. The cook for Longwood, Monsieur Lepage, is at a loss how to satisfy it."

What a vulgar man, I immediately thought, to talk of the gastric juices and the digestion of a man who for more than twenty years had shaped the history of the world. And the ostentation of the title General rather than Emperor . . . he obviously had not liked my question.

"I would be happy to meet the Emperor. Is it possible to be received by him, sir?"

"I know no Emperor on St. Helena, but if Your Imperial Highness wants to visit General Bonaparte, my governorship has no objections. I can certainly send someone to announce your arrival. I don't guarantee that he will receive you, however; he's the most eccentric man I've ever met. But he considers himself a friend of Tsar Alexander, as you can see from these notes," and he showed me, with an even more unpleasant attitude than when speaking of Napoleon's eating habits, a sheaf of letters all signed by the Emperor and never sent to the various European addresses. My eyes fell on a phrase in one of them ". . . the Emperor Napoleon is not a prisoner of war; he could have put himself into the hands of the Emperor of Russia who is his friend, or of the Emperor of Austria who is his father-in-law, but he preferred to put himself under the protection of English laws, that have his unlimited trust . . ." before I had fully realized in what the packet consisted, and handed them back, unwilling to go on reading.

I introduced him to my entourage and he introduced me to his family: a wife and daughter who I later learned were his second wife and her child from a previous marriage. I noticed he made friends immediately with Ourousov, who, by his chatter at table, freed me of the necessity to speak to the probable poisoner of Napoleon and left me to my thoughts. I was on St. Helena, a place to be remembered forever by men for the mere presence of a man. I had felt since childhood the fascination of the places to which so many men run because there a man has lived or lives alone; it seemed to me the best revenge of the one against the many, a defiance of death.

While the others at the table spoke of what were the current problems—the concordat between the King of France and the Church, the revolt in Greece, the harsh note of Russia to Turkey, the difficulties of King Ferdinand in trying to restore the ancient powers in Latin America

—I asked myself how they could be so hypocritical: if they, if we, were at that table in the governor's court, it was because Napoleon was on the island. But no one spoke of it. This silence concerning Napoleon was magnificent; it broke the back of the discussion better than would his sudden appearance under the windows, on his horse, wearing the Marengo cloak. The difference between the relating of an important historical event and a present that does not know itself to be history lay there, in the chatter of Hudson Lowe's guests on the same island, breathing the same air as Napoleon. There was room for both; the two realities traveled side by side for a long time before one reality shocked the observers that came afterward. I alone was scandalized listening to the chatter on St. Helena, I alone could not be unmoved. And I also pitied the dead at that table: two dead that chance had placed so very close to one so alive that he had to be apart from them, lest he blind them by his incapacity to die. I asked myself whether this could not be a source of pain for Napoleon, if sometimes he had not envied his jailer, the wife, the cook, the English soldiers, the Chinese who down below in the harbor of the town had welcomed us with their merchandise. That day on St. Helena I realized that it is not possible to separate the living from the dead when the dead are still living. I believe no hatred is greater than the hatred of one aware of belonging among the dead in the presence of one truly alive, as was the case of Hudson Lowe and Napoleon. There was only one way of salvation from hatred, confronted by such immense superiority, and that was love. I felt it and now, on St. Helena, I remembered how as a child at Tsarskoe Selo I had always liked to play either at being a king who commands or a servant who obeys. Watching Ourousov talking mildly with his newfound friend, I realized how childhood games foreshadow our fate.

Finally the messenger returned from Longwood with Napoleon's answer: he would receive me that same day at six o'clock in the evening.

Evidently I could not mask my excitement, because the governor came up to me and whispered confidentially: "Imperial Highness, the General is not what he was, you'll see. He's convinced he is a genius—he's lost his reason, you'll see."

I wanted to tell him that he'd finally said something intelligent, but I was no longer interested in speaking to him. I waved at him, climbed into a strange carriage drawn by six oxen and saw him lean against the column of the arcade as he waved back. I remember him thus, chained to St. Helena and to misfortune, a tragic and thoroughly forgettable figure.

It was impossible to reach Longwood, Napoleon's residence, by horse. The only vehicle was the ancient Merovingian contraption, and along the way there was nothing but a constant repetition of the same landscape: enormous rocks, frightful, bare, without a trace of vegetation, nature deranged by earthquakes. At every bend some green appeared in the distance, among some clumps of trees, but as we drew near it dissolved like a shadow: they were only seaside plants, wild dwarf shrubs, sad rubber trees. Over it all loomed the Peak of Diana, the pivot of that chain of mountains.

We arrived after two hours at a painfully slow pace. The house was poor, built quickly after they had exiled Napoleon to the island, and the smell of paint still lingered. For although the English claimed that the central wing, before the additions, had been the residence of the governor, even his servants could barely have lived there. Grand Marshal the Count of Montholon came to meet us, courteous and dry. He ushered us into a small antechamber where I was introduced to Count Las Cases, the man who had begged the honor of living near Napoleon wherever he might be sent, but who was not destined to be as faithful in his love as Hudson Lowe would be in hate.

The Grand Marshal went into Napoleon's suite to announce our arrival and returned within a few minutes: "His Majesty the Emperor awaits you, Highness."

He preceded me through one room to a door, which he opened. I was left in the doorway of a darkened room, and I saw the Emperor with his back to me, facing the truss of the hearth above which was a mirror.

"I give you my greeting, Highness. How is the Emperor Alexander?" He turned and I caught sight of my own reflection in Napoleon's mirror.

10

OUROUSOV and I arrived in Paris yesterday evening, Sunday, January 20, 1793. We slept in the Rue Saint-Honoré, not far from the square where the King will be executed today. It wasn't easy to find a place to sleep because all the Parisian hotels are full, but Ourousov can always resolve this kind of problem.

"I remember only one other occasion for a crowd as big as this: for Louis Capet when he entered Paris after the coronation," the hotel owner, Monsieur Scarron, told us last night, delighted with the brisk business. And yesterday I noticed yellow posters plastered all over the city walls, although I read them only this morning. Yesterday evening I was too exhausted by my experience on St. Helena. This morning I woke at four, before Ourousov, and went down in the street to wait for him. I read the proclamation by the Provisional Executive Council:

1. The execution of the sentence on Louis Capet will take place tomorrow, Monday 21st.

2. The place of execution will be the Square of the Revolution, once Square Louis XV.

3. Louis Capet will leave the Temple at eight o'clock in the morning, that the execution may be over by twelve noon.

4. Commissars of the Paris Municipality and two members of the court will attend the execution. The Secretary Clerk of the court and the above-mentioned delegates and members of the court will come to report to the Council as soon as the execution is over. The Council will be in extraordinary session all day.

I was fascinated not so much by the content as by the neat and restrained style that so effectively underlined the efficiency of the machinery of execution. I remembered that at Tsarskoe Selo, when the tutor Potzedonostsev taught us the French Revolution, the fact that the King was killed did not become real until the tutor recalled practical details. I would begin to follow the story when he told us the King had slept peacefully, that it was the night between Sunday and Monday, that the King had been awakened at five by Cléry, that between five and six, after the usual toilette, he had wanted to go to confession, to attend Mass and receive the Sacrament. Only when the tutor told us, talking of the toilette, that the King "had shaved" did the Revolution come alive for me, and I became attentive, absorbed in picturing the shaved cheeks of the dying King.

Looking at the poster, I felt that by the hour of death,

by midday, the King would feel the weariness consequent on the early rise. Ourousov, wrapped in his merchant's cape, caught up with me just as I finished reading the proclamation. Bourgeois cloak and dress hid our identity; it was not a day for the Russian aristocracy to visit Paris, and even less for a member of the Imperial family.

"Your Highness is surprised at the style? You should have read Cromwell's proclamation the morning of January 30th for the execution of Charles! Yes, it was January on that occasion too, but not so cold . . . the weather in Europe is changing."

There is an incredible crowd along the streets, making it difficult to move forward; like us, everyone has risen early to find a good place in the square. We have been stopped twice by boys trying to sell us a stool: thirty coins to see a unique spectacle in the history of the world. Cheap at the price. Ourousov has bought two. He seems tired, distracted. I am sure it is not always Ourousov; sometimes he absents himself, and returns to be merely my unpleasant adjutant who looks around bewildered. I have proof of it when we finally emerge into the square, at around six-thirty.

"Your Highness must excuse me, there was need of me back home; it looked as if Empress Catherine was determined to die, but something went wrong at the last moment. She'd forgotten she'd asked for a full dress rehearsal four years before the first night."

The clothes of the Frenchwomen of this period make me regret those of the women of my own time, though I am practically buried by the skirts of two women next to me—the scissors of history will bring justice to bear on the waste of so much material for a royal execution. But I cannot imagine a spectacle such as this in my day, a square so colorful, such sensual delight in a show. Amongst us in Russia, the monarchy is taken much more seriously, even on tragic occasions such as this. Our revolutionaries are grimmer, more ritualistic than the Commissars of the Municipality lined up on the platform of the guillotine, as impatient as people at table who nibble bread and wine waiting for the main course. In Russia they execute, or try to execute, as they would kill themselves, with a tragic love that seems to make the King's body their own: there is a greater mysticism, a greater consciousness of sacrifice and ritual; they are aware that they cannot destroy power with one blow to the Tsar. They are more fatalistic.

Here in France they are convinced they will change things by eliminating Louis; they do not recognize the eternal nature of power and its scandalous metamorphoses. They are happy, they do not look into the dark where the Leviathan is reborn. Coming toward the square, the young sang along the streets; but not only the young, the women, the old. And all were wearing their best clothes. I remember my grandfather's assassins; I was ten, I caught a glimpse of them on the stairs of the palace as they were being dragged away, weighed down by a sadness that here is only apparent at the top, perhaps, in leaders like Robespierre, whom I could not meet. In no square of Moscow or Petersburg will such a platform be erected for my brother. If the ogre of the fairy tale should really come, this Leonida of Ourousov's, he will be born of an evil conscience, not of a merry people such as this, for once fully participant in history.

"That Austrian woman is not with him yet, but she'll

be on trial soon." I understand French, I know they are speaking of Marie Antoinette, but I immediately think of Alix, my brother's German wife. No other woman on the throne would be less capable of understanding revolution; I know Tsarina Alexandra Feoderovna, my sister-in-law, very well.

There, the drums begin, it's a sign that Louis Capet has left the Temple and his wagon moves. I would dearly love to know what the King can be thinking on the endless journey through crowds shouting for his death. But I can imagine it, because I have never been deceived by the rejoicing crowds when I stood next to my grandfather, next to my father, behind my brother. Yet there is something of horrendous beauty in this death, in this spectacle so much greater than a coronation. Louis has never been more of a king: the wagon takes almost three hours to travel a mile. Who can judge what the cries of the people really mean when the King passes reciting the prayers of the dying? Which patricidal ghosts, never killed, awaken in their soul? The insults are an exaltation as powerful as the prayers of the King; it is a perfect chorus, with a full merging of the different voices to make a unique music. Never before has an enthroned man been able to measure so exactly the power he has had and will have as the King of France can at this time: only today can he be fully conscious that he has millions of subjects. This death is the real coronation, and Louis has never been more ter-rifying than now, when he is defenseless. Guilt will follow the people for generations, through the most liberal of governments, and will breed monsters no less repugnant than Ourousov's creatures.

Now the green wagon of the King slowly enters the square from the Rue du Faubourg Saint-Honoré. Why does the driver remind me so much of the uneasy governor of St. Helena? I am in the front row, close to the platform. They raise the blade. The wagon door is opened, the King rises to his feet and looks around at the crowd, moving his head painfully slowly. I think of Nicholas, his mild look, his beard. I shut my eyes, and for a second I see an immense flock of birds over a house into which my brother is being led with his children. On the first floor there is a deathly pale child staring out, his nose pressed against the glass. . . .

But Louis wants to talk, shouts authoritatively to the drum players to stop; and they obey the King. I want to meet his gaze now, give him my whole soul in one look; I am about to turn, to ask Ourousov for help—I do not know what is happening. . . .

"Nothing of this will be repeated in Russia," Ourousov whispers in my ear, pulling on my arm. At that moment Louis looks at me from the carriage step. And I see in the glass of the carriage window that I am weeping.

11

IN THE few minutes Ourousov had disappeared to St. Petersburg, rushing to the bedside of the great Catherine and leaving behind the old Russian Prince whose inane expression George knew only too well, things had happened at the Winter Palace that made the whole court shudder. The Empress had felt ill immediately after finishing a letter to Voltaire, who was still in touch with her, though he had been dead some years. As she replaced the quill in its stand, she had paled, her lips had twitched.

Can this be death? she wondered, and she looked at the portraits of Lisiewska and her husband and child hanging on the facing wall. She was surprised by the trembling that blurred her vision and prevented her from putting her signature on a decree that gave her name to a town in the Urals.

Let's see what happens now, she thought, and waved timidly at Saltykov with her right hand, the gesture she had always used to call her greatest favorites to her and whisper confidences. Zubov was too young; she had no need of his beauty. She needed the intelligence of Sergei, who was sixty-three, as was she.

"Maybe I'm dying, Sergei. Perhaps you should call 'him,' wherever he is."

Saltykov said nothing, but saw at a glance that he must be called. Catherine's resemblance to the proud Imperial eagle he had seen in the Caucasus Mountains, when he was with her on the campaign that annexed Georgia to the Empire, was extraordinary; now she was wearing the most arrogant, fierce and impenetrable expression a woman could wear anywhere in the world. And he knew the moment of the dress rehearsal had come, the dress rehearsal granted in the thirtieth year of her reign. Only a woman such as she on the throne could have obtained such a grace.

The force summoned by Saltykov appeared at that moment in the guise of a French courtier, murmuring, "Well, in fact, we did also grant it to Elizabeth of England." Then he spoke to the Tsarina. "Forgive the costume, Imperial Highness. We were in Paris with one of your descendants, dressed like this in front of that poor Louis," and whispered in Saltykov's ear: " . . . a bad moment for the Christian king."

"I am dying," Catherine said. "Show me what a sovereign must do at such a time," and in a few instants everything became crystal clear to her: which fictions to hand down, which truths to hide, which secrets to leave to the imagination. Her great French friend had written to her: "Remember to leave a lot to be guessed; keep yourself an enigma for posterity, and you will be seen more clearly."

Together they set down for history the official list of her forty-four lovers, then the details of her husband's murder, the anecdote of the violin, of the dog, of the Moor and his lover in the tower before they were strangled by Orlov; they allowed to remain on record the suspicions about who could have been the father of Paul, the weak-headed heir, and many other details for the delight of historians. She learned what phrases to murmur at the last moment, whom to forgive, whom to dismiss from her presence, how to behave with the Tsarevich and the Tsarina; but above all what words to whisper in the ear of her nephew Alexander, to give him the piercing memory that would arouse around her very deathbed the fatal jealousy between the unpleasant son and the beautiful nephew.

She was being prompted, directed in the dress rehearsal. She realized that it would always be a great, merely theatrical drama, even on the night when the real attack would destroy her mask; she wanted the dress rehearsal to be identical to the first night, and equally applauded.

"How easy it is . . . I would never have believed it," she whispered as he arranged her expression for the false last confession. And he thought: That's why it's easier for women . . . they have so little imagination.

She had always known that the creature preferred men to women; she had never been deluded that she could frighten him. Good agnostic that she was, she did not want her death to be anything more than theater, and her Western friends had reinforced her wish. But while her sight returned after the full dress rehearsal, she had a charming urge: she summoned her last lover, the twenty-year-old Zubov, to gaze on him now that she was coming back from death. She saw him so horrifyingly beautiful in his earthly youth that she felt in her blood all the others she had discovered and awakened with her passion. So, knowing the rehearsal was drawing to an end, she took advantage of the frivolity allowed the dying to show concern for the future of Europe.

"Nothing serious in the next century, Majesty," the creature said. "Your bloodline will still reign in the East."

"And in the West?" Catherine had loved the France of her friend Voltaire too well to forget it at that moment.

"The Republic, Majesty. That holiday for the imagination that you yourself would so much have liked."

"And then, in the century after?"

"In the West always a republic, but beyond the seas. A republic more powerful than your France. In the East no longer your blood, Majesty, but, as the agreement stipulated, some of my own creatures."

The drone of flies against the window drew her attention, and he was wrapping his cloak around himself, ready to leave. How many questions Catherine had, now that she was regaining her strength! But she handed him the letter for Voltaire, entreating him to give it to her friend.

And Ourousov was back in Paris as the hand of Catherine picked up the quill to set down her signature on the decree that gave to a town in the Urals her own name, Ekaterinburg.

12

I N THE garden of the Son of the Sky I met the most
beautiful child I had ever seen. He was playing with
paper boats as light as butterflies, and never even saw us.
He was the Emperor's son; the mask of immobility on his
grandmother's face vanished as she showed him to us, and
her expression lit up with joy.

We had reached Peking two days before, in October, 1825,
one evening when the guards were in the process of closing
the city gates at sunset. When evening falls, the divinities
that reign over China must not be distracted by the profane
activity of men and things. The streets of the city are the
veins of their body, and nothing must happen to trouble
the concentration of energies that preside at the enchantment of the Empire: the world exists because of the Emperor's ability to hold it back from its inevitable drive toward
destruction. Cities, houses, streets, walls, the fields of China

would plunge into the sea of formlessness if the Emperor were no longer granted the favor of the gods.

This became clear to me when we had seen the tomb of the Emperor, the father of the child who had played in the garden; around the tomb were buried numerous small caskets. They contained the hair of the Son of the Sky— it too a temporary manifestation of the grace of the gods —cut and kept during the thirty years of visible existence of the body to which they belonged: the Emperor had died at forty.

We were, therefore, the last visitors to be welcomed to Peking that day. I told the officials I was the nephew of the one who had sent the map of the valley that death does not reach, to say these words only to the Son of the Sky. I had not yet seen the tomb.

"Don't you know the Emperor has left? We will refer your words to the mother. And if they be not true, your head will roll."

So the Emperor was no longer in China, and the mother ruled, waiting for her son to return. Ourousov and I waited two days before being summoned to the palace. Along the way I felt as if I were crossing a city of herbs and flowers; the houses seemed ashamed of not growing like plants, and the walls were decorated with country scenes.

Ourousov noticed my absorbed contemplation of these illusory gardens: "Highness, you are puzzled, you seem not to remember this city. It's all right; on the other journey, the one you took without me, you did not manage to see it, you returned by way of Bombay."

Ourousov had become more agreeable lately, in the last

journeys. After an endless succession of halls and gardens we finally reached the Empress Mother's presence. The tall golden upraised throne made her appear more like an idol than a living goddess, a statue not yet freed of the mediation of wood and gold so necessary to become a symbol: she was merely the mother of the Emperor, not the Emperor.

"If you are looking for my son, he is on a journey. But to you, the grandson of him who gave him death, the Lord of the other half of the world, I want to tell what I will announce tomorrow: my son is dead. Tell your father's father when you reach him after your head falls to the bottom of the pit. Because you will atone for the deception that made us lose him."

She then told us how her son had waited years for the man who had promised him the map of the other side of the world, how he walked every day along the streets of the palace complex to the tower where he and the man had spoken their last farewell. "His eyes were consumed with looking to the West," she said, "while his enemies devastated the country in the East. He let me make all the decisions, and I could not because I am a woman. So I made him sleep with the most beautiful women to distract him. He had to have a son; only thus could he and China be saved from his disease. A child was born and the Emperor seemed to waken to a new life, seemed to forget his watch and to conquer the enemies of our light.

"I was already preparing my own tomb, and he had not been to the tower for many months when, one day, the man from your country returned. The Emperor was administering justice in this very hall, with his son, and the man was there, where you are now. The Emperor recognized him at a glance, and without even bringing to an end what he was doing, he went to meet him and gave him his hand. The man had with him the map from your father's father. My son wanted it immediately, and ordered us to withdraw at once. I begged for days and nights, weeping with the mother of the child. I implored him in vain to show us the map, to allow explorers to go ahead, not to trust the other Emperor. He left with twenty men, picked carefully in the land where all the rivers of the Empire have their source, promising them that they would reach the gods in those mountains.

"He left his son, his son's mother and me with the order not to wait for him, indifferent whether we would declare him dead or would announce he was on a journey and would return. 'In any case,' he told me, 'I will be dead for you, for my son and his mother. I want my death in death.'

"He has not returned, and China is so big we have received reports of him being sighted in seven provinces already. Seven Emperors claim to be father of the child. I had to erect the tomb you will see before you die. China would have died if I had not decided to announce his death and proclaim his son Emperor."

I refrained from telling her that a man had sacrificed himself so that nothing worse might happen, so that her son and Alexander could believe that what they searched for was in their Empire, within their reach. It was not the man's fault that they had not understood and had believed the other face of the mirror.

The Emperor's mother summoned the guards with a motion of her fingers. "Three things you must see before you die," she said to me. We went through paths and lawns to the pond where I saw the most beautiful child in the world, singing with a voice of such enchantment I had to close my eyes. But an insistent twittering forced me to open them immediately: the child was fashioning birds out of mud, and as he finished each he blew on it and it took flight, without however flying too far away from him. And in that instant I saw again the house to which Nicholas was being taken and the pale child at the window.

But already the soldiers were coming to take us to the grave of the Emperor, the tomb that contained only death, and had to be dwelt in from tomorrow if China was to be saved. "All that you can imagine has already been" was the inscription which Ourousov translated for me. Then the Empress made us climb a parapet; from there we could see the wide foundations of a temple with ample stairways. The walls were painted, alive, full of movement, and as I drew near I could observe the figures more closely: they were men and women of various shapes and sizes, in the poses of love, in a joyous celebration of their strength and beauty. We walked around for a long time, followed by the guards. No two scenes were alike; each hid a different mystery.

"Now you can die. Take him to the pit," was the order. Next to the pit all was ready. The executioner toyed with the axe. In the water at the bottom I saw that my eyes were still absorbed by the vision of the men and women in the Temple of Love.

13

W E ARE in Rome, in the antechamber to the
office of Cardinal Ercole Consalvi, the Secretary
of State of the Roman Pontiff. It is the morning of May 17,
1818. The butler has just announced our presence, but the
Cardinal appears to be in no hurry to receive us.

"Rome is not an open society, Imperial Highness," Ourousov says. "It will be difficult to remain more than a few
hours . . . but for centuries now I've had more enjoyment
in Rome than in any other city of the world. Even Luther
noticed it when he came here as a young man."

Ourousov paces up and down in front of the door to
the office and explains that the prelate is very worried
because he doesn't know who I am, what the precise re-
lationship is to Tsar Alexander I. He has searched through
the directory of heralds but in the pages reserved to the
Romanovs, before the Rosenbergs and Rospigliosi, he found

three blank pages, and feels it cannot be a mistake on the part of the Florentine printers. He has called Prince Borghese to have lunch with him; the Prince knows the Tsar well, perhaps he can be of some help.

"A bad morning for the poor Cardinal," Ourousov continues. "He has received a letter this very morning from Tsar Alexander. It's on his desk, personally signed by him, and it's been doing the rounds of the Curia for the last month. It's a renewal of the entreaty that the Pope join the Holy Alliance, and Pius VII doesn't feel like sitting side by side with a Protestant, an Orthodox and a Catholic. He doesn't understand what the consequences might be for such an alliance; he senses heresy and is not altogether mistaken."

The door of the office opens and we are ushered into the presence of His Eminence. The study is in shadow against the early heat of this Roman spring, and the large room of the seventeenth-century palace, with its tall paneled ceiling, is pleasantly cool.

The Cardinal speaks perfect French in a thin voice: "Imperial Highness, Prince, I have the honor of welcoming you in the name also of my Sovereign, the Roman Pontiff."

"Our gracious thanks, Eminence. It is a pleasure to visit Rome. His Imperial Highness has never been." Ourousov answers in Italian, with a slight inclination of the head, and looks at me.

I smile at the Cardinal, whose old lined face is familiar; I feel as if I've already met him, but I don't know where. He's tense, though he tries to hide it. The gnarled arthritic hands move constantly to tidy and change the position of objects on the desk, the pens, the blotters, the hourglass, the full and the empty inkwells.

He speaks again: "It is a city full of history and beauty. I shall be pleased to unlock some of its secrets for His Imperial Highness."

"But His Imperial Highness is here not only for cultural reasons, as Your Eminence has in all probability already guessed. . . ." Ourousov makes an effort to hide his glance at the desk where the folder with the Tsar's letter lies.

Consalvi fidgets in the chair; moving objects is no longer enough. He is obviously annoyed at my silence.

"Truly we cannot guess the reason for the honor of your visit, of your presence here in Rome. . . . If Your Highness could let us know more precisely, we will be only too pleased to do whatever is possible and within the power of our government to satisfy his wishes." And the Cardinal looks at me encouragingly.

But Ourousov interposes in his all-too-correct Italian: "It is a delicate question, as we are well aware. And we can only touch on it, since in half an hour Prince Camillo Borghese is due to arrive. However, it would be to the Pope's great benefit if he could perform some preliminary work on a question that will bring difficulties in eighty-one years' time."

Now the Cardinal cannot hide his tension, leans back in the chair and rises, tall and gaunt. He stares insistently at the communicating door of the study.

"Don't be alarmed, Eminence," Ourousov says, smiling. "There is no need to call the guards. Grand Duke George is here to renounce the crown of Poland. He is immensely grateful to the Pontiff and begs you to convey his gratitude to him, but he cannot accept the sovereignty of that unfortunate country. He cannot speak, because he's yet unborn, but he understands your French perfectly."

At these words Cardinal Ercole Consalvi grabs the arms of the tall chair behind him and moves it violently aside.

The smiling Ourousov continues in a mocking voice: "Even though the Grand Duke is not yet born, he is already resolved not to head the Polish rebellion against his brother Nicholas II. As for you, Eminence, who will be dead for seventy-five years, it is to your advantage to know the answers to the delicate questions of the future, that your Florentine descendants may add foresight to the praise of your other talents—to be inscribed in Latin on your tomb at St. Peter's next to that of Pius VII: '*Restitutor fidei Polonorum; defensor Ecclesiae.*' "

"*Vade retro, vade retro, Satana,*" and the Cardinal Secretary of State of the Holy Roman Church, wildly reciting prayers, backs toward the door until he reaches the great baroque mirror, where finally I can see all my reflections. Only now do I have the strength to step into the mirror and fully penetrate my own image.

And I am still in Rome a century before, the youngest Cardinal in conclave. It is the first day, the day before the first rounds of votes. We are still all asleep in our cells; the Holy Spirit has whispered the name of the future Pope into the ear of my brothers in Christ. I would not yet have waked up if a little white bird had not come to my windowsill to sing. The sun is already high over Rome. The great silence convinces me I am the only one awake.

And if the other Cardinals were dead? I shudder. I am

Pope, and in a little while I have to declare it to the world. Will the world believe me?

I stand, irresolute, listening to the little bird chirping joyously, praying that the song will halt time and wipe out the day, that I can remain in the night of my cell forever; and I don't notice that the Cardinals have already gathered in the Sistine Chapel. Ourousov comes to call me as I am searching my pockets for some crumbs to give the little bird. I must go. I am the next Pope.

It seems that I went on searching my pockets while they clothed me in white in front of another mirror with five lights, a little before I left it to return to my own time.

14

THEY returned to Abas-Tuman with difficulty, coming in at the wrong time. Ourousov had lost the
way back, but George suspected the adjutant wanted to
distract him, convince him to forget the Empire, his title,
the illness, Helen, to wander forever in time, writing what
he dictated.

"Imperial Highness, now we will return to your brother's
reign, but don't lose heart, sometimes these returns are so
disappointing as to be mistaken for errors. . . . You, Highness, will return to your century when you truly want to."

So they returned to Russia at eight o'clock in the morning
on the seventh of November, 1938. They were standing on the
side of the stream where Adam's isba had been; in its place
there was a human beehive, ten floors high, made of dark
brick. It hummed with life at that hour. George, walking
along the street, could hear the cry of the women, the voices

of the husbands, the slamming of doors, a confused buzzing that was at moments transformed into song.

"Radios, Highness," Ourousov explained to the puzzled George; "boxes that can reproduce voices even at a distance of a thousand versts. Most people use them not to listen to anyone, but not to be alone and forced to think."

"Who invented it?"

"An Italian, apparently. And one day they'll find an even more efficient instrument to stop people from thinking, Highness. It will come from America, it will be a luminous object that reproduces images at a distance."

"Like the magic lantern."

"In a way."

Abas-Tuman seemed totally changed. It had been transformed into a big center full of smoldering, smoking chimneys. There were cars on the roads, and where once it had been a pleasure to walk it was now difficult.

"Yes, Highness, this fetid air comes from the chimneys that provide food for practically the whole country."

"What do they produce?"

"Cars and death. The cars the government would like to export, but they work badly. The factories also make agricultural machinery and clothing machinery, and all the time the poison from the chimneys kills the people little by little."

They went toward the first bar they saw, on the corner of the street.

"Highness, beware any political talk. Never . . ."

George looked at him, surprised; since when did a member of the Imperial family engage in political talk? They went in. Everyone drank, standing, with the haste of the pursued, not speaking to each other. Where was the friendly noise of the bar he had loved to frequent, to immerse himself in the strong sweet odors of tobacco and vodka? He looked at the young man at the counter and ordered two vodkas: it was certainly Petya's son, he looked so much like his father. But without his father's artful calm. They left, and George proposed going up to the castle. As they began the climb, Ourousov grew thoughtful, searching for the right words to say to the Grand Duke.

"Imperial Highness, the castle is no longer a castle; your family no longer comes here to vacation. Now it's an office, like many other Imperial palaces. The most beautiful buildings have been turned into offices, archives and museums."

The slope amongst the trees he had so often trudged up and down was lined with numerous identical three-story houses, each one with its little garden and minute pond, its three flower beds and gate. The women beating rugs on one side of the slope were identical to the women on the other side, hurrying through their chores to go to the factory and make cars that worked badly and caused death. The gray overalls, the bearskin caps, the heavy furs, the pale faces, drawn from lack of sleep, gave the climb a quality of nightmare from which George hoped to wake at the castle. As he walked, he asked himself what had happened to his family, but the advantage of writing was in the deceptive perception of events, a constant irony that took away credibility from every landscape and phenomenon.

Perhaps only a dream so crowded with events that a thousand nights were not enough to tell them would show any resemblance to the adventure he was writing. He was learning a new indifference toward himself and those he loved. An attitude of calculated moral apathy and lascivious memory he'd never experienced before. As if living were only remembering, remembering even the new to imprint it in the memory and therefore immediately kill it. He was no longer certain when he wanted to return home to his own time. He had become a kind of workman of memory: to produce the past, working as little as possible in the present, to save the consciousness of his illness by an expansion of the imagination that was ever greater and always less careful not to damage itself.

Perhaps even those he loved, starting with Helen, would understand his need to forget them in order to find them. Looking at Ourousov walking by his side, he wondered whether this outpost of the journey was not Ourousov's last attempt to lose him in one of the most tortuous labyrinths of the soul; the illness that had gnawed at him for years was all there, in the face of the faithful servant, in that game of truancy he himself was playing with those who had been calling out to him for who knows how long to lay down the pen and return. What harm was there in such a journey, in such a return to distant points, in the egotism of remembering? Was he still alive on this day, or was he already dead? What time was this? A memory of his real future, or an arrogant dislocation granted by time, an arbitrary tear in the future? He still had a few French coins in his pocket, given him by the French hotel owner, Monsieur Scarron. They were more distressing even than the rows of identical houses where the lives of those freed from his brother's dominion were being lived out.

Because, of course, his brother was no more. Ourousov

had not wanted to tell him, and he had not wanted to know, but Nicholas II was no more. Knowledge of the Tsar's own story, the story of the last Tsar, was a weight too heavy for George to bear. To reconstruct his own story, of the younger brother, was burden enough. Another slow progress came to his mind as they made their slow way to the castle: the even-paced rolling advance of Louis XVI's green carriage toward the guillotine while the King prayed the prayers of the dying with a clarity so rarely granted. A king even at those moments. And Nicholas? Had he endured the perception of what was happening as Louis had, or was he spared it? In Paris, observing the King, Ourousov had said that nothing of what he saw would happen to Russia. It must have happened differently. Only prisoners condemned to languish for life in a fortress, losing all knowledge of the passing days in boredom, or the inmates of an insane asylum who lose their sense of time in madness, could equal the royal bearing George had seen in the mirrors. Yes, he thought, only the Siberian prisons which disgorged none but those on their way to the cemetery or to the asylums of Moscow—only they could glow with the dark splendor of the mirrors.

At a bend in the road they came upon the post office, and George looked curiously at the crest on the door. The star was beautiful, the star that other men on earth had emblazoned to symbolize their hope. But why the hammer and sickle? For what did the state stand? If the sickle on its own could be a symbol of the labor of time and civilization, next to the hammer it took on a different meaning, free from the ambivalence ineluctably linked to labor, hardship, travail.

"It's the symbol of work, in fact," Ourosov whispered, and George, still walking, closer now to the castle, wondered how a state could use labor as a symbol of its essence; was it not a curse in the Bible? One of the two absolute limitations, the other being birth itself, the painful entry into existence—bestowed on man and woman after their sin of arrogance? How could one live by putting at the very center of one's existence the limits to be transcended? Was toil itself the reason for toil? George could not understand. That society, which must exist all over the Empire, as it manifested itself in Abas-Tuman, forbade itself to transcend life, to impress on it a different direction, one beyond, out among the stars. What star could glow for a chained world without giving any hope that the chains could be broken? He had found himself at a point in history too removed from his existence. He was already dead, because death only took place when change could no longer be understood.

They had reached the castle. On the great entrance door the same coat of arms, but bigger; under it was still visible the outline of the Imperial eagle. The sentry boxes on either side stared vacantly out; obviously there was no one to guard a building where citizens hurried to and fro. He went in and joined a queue, getting in place before Ourousov. Thirty-eight years before, in that selfsame hall, they would have had to stand to attention with a sharp clicking of the heels. Ourousov's rooms had been on the ground floor, next to those of the Grand Duke's secretary; now those rooms were offices, and on the doors stood clearly the iron signs "BIRTH CERTICATES," "CERTICATES OF WIDOWHOOD," "DEATH CERTICATES": certificates of existence.

Without realizing it, he had put himself into the proper

queue, the one for the death certificates. Through that door were the kitchens. . . . Few people in line, at the most twenty; they would be done in no time. While he waited, he looked at the faces of his Georgians, the onetime faithful subjects, and they still seemed the same, fearful to meet his eyes in the marketplace as soon as Ourousov had caught sight of them. Now the widows and the old looked at him blankly, but their eyes lit up when they saw Ourousov.

Finally, George reached the window: "I'd like my death certificate. I am Grand Duke George Alexandrovich Romanov."

"What'd you say, comrade?"

"I'd like my death certificate. My name is George Alexandrovich Romanov."

"Have you put in a request?" the clerk asked, barely leaning forward.

"This is the first time."

"Then you must go to another office—second floor, fourth door on the right."

The door to my suite, George thought, following Ourousov up the wide staircase where no hussar stood at attention. How the house had changed . . . only people, busy putting in requests for their papers, officials and doormen everywhere. Everywhere the stench of cigarettes, impregnating the walls, the curtains, the faded writing of directions on the stairs. Stubs everywhere, dirty windows, ceilings full of cobwebs the cleaning staff obviously could not reach. And who in any case could care for such an anonymous place, a place merely to come to, to withdraw forms designed to prove your existence for the state? No life was lived any longer within the state since all lives were subsumed in it. And yet what endless smoke in that room where there was no longer one life to give weight to the existence of many.

"Is it here that one asks for a death certificate if one has not yet died?" Ourousov asked the doorman in a humble voice.

"Yes, comrade, if you mean the first request."

"Yes."

"Well, join the queue."

George looked at his rooms: the antechamber, the study, the bedroom were the offices from which his death certificate would be issued. His death had been born in those rooms as intimately as any habit. But where were the beautiful paintings? The chandeliers, carelessly left alight all the time, had lost many of their crystals. A man was busy trying to free himself of a person who, in George's day, would have been a petitioner, and was now, like everyone else, "comrade."

"I can't do anything about it, Krapugin, you'll have to come back in a week, after the meeting of the Abastumani Soviet."

"But, Comrade Director, it's so easy, it won't take a minute . . . all it needs is a signature."

"Really, Krapugin, it's out of the question before the meeting of the Central Committee. You can't know what they think of it in Moscow, and I certainly don't—can't you understand?"

And the director rushed on through those corridors, which must have appeared spellbinding to the poor Krapugin, who stared around as if his very life depended on what they contained. George felt a moment of compassion, knowing so well that those rooms were empty. For the first time since the onset of the journey, he wished to be who he was, son of and brother to the Tsars, just to open doors for the likes of poor Krapugin, even if it was only to grant him the grace of exile in Siberia.

"Careful, don't think like that; it shows. You'll have time for acts of mercy if they give us the blessed certificate," Ourousov whispered. It was their turn.

"What's the name of the dead one, comrade?" If he was there, how could he put in the request? George asked himself.

"George Alexandrovich Romanov."

"Date of death?"

"June 20, 1899," Ourousov muttered faintly. George did not hear; Helen was on the other side of the hall, standing in front of a window. It was Helen. George rushed across to her side trembling.

He touched her arm and she turned, saying gently, "What is it, comrade?"

". . . Nothing, nothing, I mistook you for someone else." How could that common woman look so much like her from behind? How many women had he noticed that day walking through Abas-Tuman who had the same strong features? What had come over him? He staggered back to the queue where Ourousov was waiting for him, leaning, completely relaxed, against the wall next to the window.

"Highness, we have to come back in two days' time. Meanwhile we can go on a little, before coming back. Or would you rather wait here in Abas-Tuman? There's a hotel in town—the manager will find us two rooms even if we don't have documents on us at the moment."

"I'm tired, Prince. I don't like seeing people in my house, nor do I want to see people in a hotel. I don't want to stay here and I don't want to move on. I want to listen to someone who will make me forget this story of mine."

"As you wish, Highness. Let's go, then."

And they left by the same route they had taken when everything began, when he had given the order of departure one morning without saying for how long he would be gone. He saw again the paths he had taken through the mountains, thinking of Alexander after Adam's words. The Elbrus appeared in all its majesty, and George was conscious again of how those mountains knew nothing of time present and time past, knew less than nothing of his story within history.

He was still troubled by the vision of Helen. He saw a sparrow sway on a branch: its weight, however slight, was able to bring about a union, though it might last less, even, than his fleeting sight of bird and branch, and less than the illusion that had distracted him when she had appeared to him at home, in the house where he had never yet seen her. Now the bird flapped its wings and took flight, just as the false Helen had when she had turned and left him to his solitude. The branch no longer swayed; it had begun waiting once more.

But someone was coming toward them down the mountains. Two people who laughed and joked. One voice was not new, and George was startled; he had heard it many times as a boy. Michael, the youngest brother, their father's favorite, was coming toward him along the path, followed by another young man. He felt immediately that he was still alone, that for Michael everything was as it had always been: he, George, was the melancholy and eccentric sick brother who lived in the Caucasus, to whom he had last spoken in October from Orel. Prince Ourousov bowed to Grand Duke Michael, the most probable heir.

"Have you heard, George? Another girl! Poor Nicholas. And Alix is distraught, won't let herself be seen by anyone, didn't even want to receive me when I went to congratulate them. She suspects I merely wanted to tease her because she had not bestowed an heir and that I would be happy to be confirmed in my position. So you hadn't heard?"

"Imperial Highness, forgive the interruption, but we've been traveling for some days."

Was Ourousov afraid he had not understood that Michael had no connection to his story? That his brother lived in a completely different narrative? Behind Michael and a little to the side, in an attitude of respectful attention, was an extremely good-looking young man—probably a foreigner, because he had the smiling, lost air of someone who wants to please though he doesn't understand what is being said. So George was greatly surprised when the man greeted him in the most faultless Russian he had ever heard. Who was he, so ready to identify with whomever he was with?

"He's a poet, George. I've given him my hope never to die; when I am no more, the poetry he dedicates to me will continue. He has a power not even Nicholas has. I often go to the theater in Petersburg masked in a thousand ways so that I may not be recognized. I discovered him one night when he was acting in one of his plays, a play too beautiful for our unfortunate times. I'd love him to act some of it out for you, but he won't, he's embarrassed; he's not yet aware of the power he has—" Michael stopped as if to allay a suspicion, then began in a higher-pitched voice: "Do you think you're the only one who's afraid of dying? What am I saying? It's desire for life, not fear of death, my dear George. We are insatiable, and you've found the excuse of illness to persuade death to give you two lives in exchange for one, the common life. I have found no one but him. I have riches, health, freedom to marry the greatest princesses of Europe, my parents are among the potentates of the earth. But I have nothing—or, at least, I had nothing until I met him. I don't know where, how but sometimes when he writes, when he speaks and we're alone together, he has words that linger, that I feel I've always known. He's young and soon, very soon, he'll realize his power; he'll love others, he'll have success, wives, children, money, and lose everything in pursuit of what will be of no use to him."

George wanted to tell him that the words the young man seemed to send beyond death had no power to halt even an instant of life, that within words such as "summer" and "love" there is a scent that is as ephemeral as that of freshly baked bread. Michael seemed to read his thoughts, took him by the hand and drew him to the beautiful stranger, who smiled at him as if he wanted to speak, and George saw in the smile the world: the ethereal dome, the earth with its mountains, continents, oceans, the wind, the fire, the moon, the stars and, in the end, himself amongst the Caucasus Mountains. He shuddered, lowered his gaze, bewildered, and took a step back nearer to Ourousov, who sat on a rock apart and looked at the Elbrus at sunset.

He came out of his vertigo at Michael's words: "Your Ourousov is a strange old man. A patriarch gazing at the sunset over the promised land," and, smiling mischievously, Michael turned to his young friend. "Kolia's been enchanted too."

The young man did not appear to know they were talking about him; he seemed interested only in Ourousov. George felt again the anguish that he had felt the day of Ourousov's transfiguration, and looked around. Of course: they had stopped for the night at precisely this point after the stag had disappeared. Then too the sun had set and everything had begun. At that moment he understood that his brother was lost too, that Michael's young poet was the same power that had deluded him into writing that journey in time. Michael could not see what George saw in the young man's eyes as he looked at the old man, a conspiratorial glint so similar to that in Monsieur Scarron's eyes, in the eyes of Louis XVI's coachman, of his own personal doctor, of Hudson Lowe on St. Helena, of hundreds of ministers throughout time.

"Oh, Michael!" The cry escaped him, but a glance from Ourousov pulled him back and he did not finish. They were lost: he, Michael and probably Nicholas too, the Tsar, there in his palace at St. Petersburg, where an Ourousov could so easily hide. What a perennial battle between one power and another—battles enacted everywhere, as they were here, in the shadow of Mount Elbrus being enveloped by night. But the snow still shone in the darkness.

When they separated and Michael and his friend left,

George felt the full sadness of a fading vision, an illusion as all the others had been on the journey. He told Ourousov he was ready for his death certificate, and in a few minutes they were again on the second floor of the castle, standing before the clerk of the office.

15

"OMRADE, there is no George Alexandrovich Romanov in our town. Are you sure of the date?"

"Certainly—how can it be?" George answered.

"But no one of this name has died here in the last twenty
years."

So his death must have occurred before or after that
time, but George did not want to know; he wanted to go
back to where it had all started.

Ourousov interrupted: "Can we speak to the director?
We had special information on this case."

After a good half hour they were ushered into the study
of the director, Ivan Petrovich Zeljabov. "Who is George
Alexandrovich Romanov?" the director asked.

George saw again the library, the tables, the shelves; the
glass stands with his coin collection that was no more. A
big portrait of a man in uniform, wearing an obtrusive
mustache, had been hung next to the coat of arms of star,

sickle and hammer, in the exact spot where once stood the showcase with the Spanish coins, the most beautiful pieces of his collection.

"His Imperial Highness, second son of Alexander III. Here he is, Comrade Ivan Petrovich. He's twenty-eight and he wants his own death certificate," Ourousov answered indifferently. "You try if you can to convince him it's not worth persisting."

"Who allowed you to come in and waste my time? That fool Nicolai . . . Do you think you can play such tricks on me with impunity? I'll show you . . . Anton! Anton!" The furious director stood up, calling the doorman.

"But, Director, why not make a new certificate? What do you lose? I died here, probably in the room beyond that door, where my bedroom was. Do you really not have the papers of the Imperial administration?"

"The Imperial administration? The son of the Tsar? Where do you spring from? I'll have you put in jail immediately. These are nostalgics, Whites, counterrevolutionaries! Oh, I'll fix you, see if I don't . . . Anton! Anton!"

But Anton didn't come and the director worked himself up into a frenzy of revolutionary ardor, quoting phrases by a man who was in all probability the mustachioed man of the portrait.

"Siberia, Siberia for people like you. He said it: 'Watch and be on guard, there will be a wave of counterrevolutionaries.' He knows Georgia well, he was born amongst these mountain people."

So his Georgia had given birth to the new Tsar; so Georgians really were different from all the other populations of the Empire. He had always known the little nation would one day reawaken, would show forth the new Tsar. . . . "And you, Bethlehem, are not the last among the lands of Judah. . . ."

"Really the new Tsar is from Georgia?" he asked almost timidly, as if it could not possibly be true, wanting confirmation. And all the time he stared at the great photograph on the wall. Where had he seen those long ratlike whiskers before, that strange animal grin? And why as he gazed on it did he feel as if he were losing his foothold? But Anton had still not appeared. The director kept ringing the bell in vain, in vain kept shouting the Polish name of the usher. Anton would not come. In his place, George's sleepy valet turned up, obviously sent up from Livadia to Abas-Tuman before the Grand Duke himself moved to Georgia. At the sight of his master in strange clothes, the valet stood speechless, not knowing what to think. And who was that person behind the desk? George saw the bewilderment on the face of the official and finally remembered where he had seen the face of the photograph: it was the foul creature who had hugged Ourousov's legs with its fins in the Caucasus Mountains. By now the room of the Director of Registers in Abastumani, a town in the Socialist Republic of Soviet Georgia, was floating like an isle set adrift from the great peninsula in a huge earthquake. The room—with its electric bell, the desk, the filing cabinets, typewriters, the portrait of Stalin, the heraldic star, hammer and sickle and the worthy official—had become the castle of Tsar Nicholas's brother Grand Duke George Alexandrovich Romanov, in the middle of the year 1899.

George was home. The doctor was waiting to make the usual evening visit. In a flash Ourousov froze Ivan Petrovich

Zeljabov in his pose, hands in the air and mouth open, and compelled him to wait for Anton in that rhetorical position, to wait thirty-eight years, four months and nine days. Ourousov closed the door of Zeljabov's regime and personally sealed it: a large tapestry of the sleeping, snake-haired Medusa dropped over the door and was never spoken of again. Let the officials look more carefully in the Abastumani of the future to discover who the second son of Alexander III might be, let them find the death certificate of the Grand Duke.

"The cruise was pleasant, Imperial Majesty? Your Highness looks a little tired, but with no fever," the doctor said, feeling George's pulse. But George knew by now who the doctor was; he was tired of pretending. He closed his eyes without replying. A little later he was left alone, in his home, in his room, in his time. As he had so often done before, he delighted in the scent of the sheets and the pillowcase while the light, filtered as it always had through the shutters, drew the same shapes against the walls. The present was such a fragile shell, squeezed by such strong powers: it had to be loved, no longer avoided, no longer fled from; he had to become a citizen of his brother's Empire, to give the present his trust and save it from being condemned.

In the house, meanwhile, the powers waged their war. The room of the Soviet official, behind the arras of the Medusa, waited for the breath of air of the seventh of November, 1938. The darkness knew that Anton, the Polish doorman, would answer the summons of Ivan Petrovich; the dust that settled on the nose and hands of the comrade director held the same guarantee of time as that which blackened the coins in George's pockets, the coins to pay the bill for a meal on that cold Sunday, the twentieth of January, 1793, in Paris. Bean soup, rissoles, potatoes, walnut cheese, Burgundy wine—seventy-two sous of the mint in year One of the Republic. Such was the sum marked on the bill at the hotel on the Rue Saint-Honoré. To which dimension did that meal belong? To historical time, to the time of the French Revolution or to the devil's time, to the time of George's long journey written under dictation from one of the "I"s who had slid into reality from the mirror? On the table lay the broken quill that had belonged to Byron. The labors of the story, of History, subsided in the sleep of the ailing Grand Duke, reconciling the languishing Empire of his brother to all the powers that the prerogatives of the imagination had allowed him to substitute for the actual powers of an autocrat.

Sleep, sleep alone could permit Nicholas to face the revolution. No one apart from Ourousov would ever know that the first revolution, the one that was to break out only six years hence, would be decided in favor of the Tsar on that night, in the sleep of a brother, the ailing Grand Duke who had gone to gather his forces in Georgia, looking for the valley where there is no death. The Romanov family was to draw on that capacity to suffer and endure death, in order to beat death and delay its arrival at least by the number of years one of its heirs had had to wait for it.

16

HELEN had come. But George did not know it: they had been waiting for some sign of reawakening for three days. In vain: his face looked so serene in sleep that it was difficult to imagine he would want to return to the wakeful state.

Helen had arrived one morning, had been received by Ourousov and an official of the Grand Duke's personal corps. She had left the carriage as if in a dream, had looked around slowly. She had spoken to Ourousov immediately: the first obstacle to overcome was the courtier whom Nicholas had placed with his brother. She did not know him except by letter; she had never seen him. The last time, in Livadia, Ourousov had gone to Petersburg for the birth of a son. Watching the Prince, she began to understand why George's last letters had been so obscure. The man was a model of all Russian courtiers, as unctuous and untrustworthy, obliging and false, solicitous and double-dealing as it was possible to be. She understood why her George, exhausted by illness and solitude, had ended by endowing him with all sorts of powers of machination. She understood what it meant to be a servant: she had never seen its manifestation so clearly. There was no autonomy in the man: phrases, advice, exhortations, his constant apologies, his oblique revelations, the half smiles that changed to grimaces, all his being, his voice—these were only under-standable in the context of a greater reality from which they drew their strength. There was in every expression a perennial auxiliary, like the auxiliary in the verbs of many European languages—such as the active and passive forms that the verbs "to be" and "to have" gave to a sense of things achieved. He was servant, and was servile, auxiliary to another who had him in his power. Yes, there was no greater power than the terror to which Prince Ourousov was heir. His will did not exist; the man was as free of it as if he had lost it from all eternity. He did not even seem a man, his way of being was so distant from the word "will" and from the other word, so full of historical nuances, the word "freedom."

Certainly the Tsar could see in him the most faithful servant. But if Helen remembered the mild Nicholas II while she listened to the whining details of Ourousov, she had to recognize that the need of the servant to obey was greater by far than the need of the master to command. Neither Tsar nor Emperor of China would be able to assuage his thirst to obey, his hunger for dependence. When they finished speaking, she realized that nothing had changed, no decision had been made, no new fact had come to light.

She could not say whether Ourousov would in fact tell the Tsar, if the man would help her by not revealing her presence in Abas-Tuman. She decided not to dwell on it; she understood that the real master for Ourousov was her own fear of him. So she ordered him not to speak until she herself had told the Tsar, and then left Ourousov not a moment of rest, giving him a whole series of commands and duties that came to her more and more clearly as she crossed halls and rooms.

This was George's home? So neglected? It looked as if it had been uninhabited for a century, or lived in by someone who was constantly away, never here. It certainly was not a home fit for the brother of the Tsar. Didn't he know the Tsar intended to spend a week here in a month's time? And could this be the dwelling place of her cousin even for one night? She complained about the deplorable state of the guest quarters, especially the suite Ourousov thought she would grace with her presence. The marigolds had withered, had not been watered for at least forty-eight hours. Didn't they realize these were flowers that should have water every day?

There was not a room that did not become subject to the severe scrutiny of Helen's black eyes; the cook, the scullery staff, the coachman, the maids and house boys, the valets, the stable boys, even the soldiers of the guard corps were criticized while George's sleep continued, and Helen did not consider it advisable to interrupt it after the stress of the cruise, which, she knew from a letter of the Tsar, had lasted quite a number of days. There was not one room she did not go into, seized by a fervor that led her to examine everything that came under Ourousov's jurisdiction. Meanwhile she felt the snowbound Elbrus watching her, looking in on her through the windows; as she climbed from the first to the other floors, the mountain made her feel that the neoclassical building was too low, as if there were not enough floors. The house should have risen to the sky, that more could be given back new to George after being handled by her. Toward evening she ended her complaints to the Prince, to the doctor, to the officer of the guards about the deplorable state of the Imperial residence by threatening to refer to the Tsar the culpable negligence and carelessness of the man on whom Nicholas had put so much trust for over ten years.

Then he too understood that he was the most disgusting servant that could live in a court. She watched him lose all dignity and cry like a child, sobbing with a sincerity that bewildered her. This man could really only legitimatize himself through a master, or his strength would be completely extinguished and he would suffer total dissolution. On what could such primitive servitude depend? Helen still looked up at the great mountain whose top was hidden by clouds. She asked herself who had ever seen its top in this house that seemed to have been built just for such a contemplation.

At night she withdrew into George's rooms and all was peace. Sitting in his armchair next to the bed, she listened to the house she had so often imagined, even the remotest corner of which was now devoid of all secrets. She had been surprised when Ourousov, after wiping his tears, had handed her the keys to a secret room behind an arras on the first floor, in case she wanted to visit it too.

"It's not a room I'm interested in; you can keep the key, you can take care of it," she told him.

She did not know why she had immediately reacted thus, without thinking, instinctively. She had reacted in the same way when she and her parents had found themselves in the United States within a matter of minutes: there were boundaries she wanted to respect, things she did not want to know; sometimes it was too early to understand. Things happened that did not honor the speed of the mind; few were trained for them. Yet they occurred. She had left to her mother and father, once they returned to Russia, the advantage of religion, of dreams, of illness—all the possible ways to accept the inexplicable that man so expertly provides for himself. She knew there should be a strategy against certain offensive actions, even if one did not know the reasons for such offenses. Perhaps they were not even offenses or acts of violence, but in the meantime it was essential to react because sight, hearing, all the senses were still accustomed to animals, marigolds, men who walked. Men progressed too slowly: those on the other side gained ever stronger positions; every day some crucial strategic position was lost; the war was carried out carelessly, lazily, without room for hope. And yet why was it that despite its overwhelming superiority, the advancing enemy could not deliver the final blow? The world had been a miracle of survival for thousands of years. Weakness, terror, imperfection clouded everything, yet everything remained: new troops replaced the old, rescue always came at the last minute. And they, the conquerors, could never say they had finally managed to uproot these races. They were the conquerors, certainly, we the conquered. But the war had never ended. And George's sleep, which had lasted too many hours, now seemed to her another defense against those enemies, a defense that had to be respected. She would wait for him to wake, happy to stay as guard of his sleep and watch over him.

She looked at the desk crowded with papers, but she did not want to read those pages black with his minute script, where the cross-outs and the spots of ink still seemed to compete with thought.

In the profound silence of the house she extinguished the light. George slept on. This was what she still had to believe, but in reality where was George? Where could his laughter be heard, what landscape did his green eyes behold? What did he see now, he who had been so eager to recognize life before it had even taken shape? Where was he being led by the weakness that had put him under poor Ourousov's domination for so long? What events would the weakness of its Prince create in the history of Russia? What monsters had the illness fashioned during her absence, while she was far away and struggling to come to him? Which intrigue was already impossible to overcome, even with the whole strength of her love? She did not know what had taken place behind the sleeping forehead, but she had to wage war against furies already unleashed and free. One more time she had to prepare to fight enemies that were more ancient and threatening than an enemy at the borders of Russia. Neither Turks nor Chinese, neither Tatars nor Mongols would ever have the power that Ourousov had usurped from this Prince of one of the most ancient families in Europe.

She started to pray that the sleep be a healing sleep: perhaps the balance of many nations within Europe depended on it, perhaps two or three future wars would retreat back into the minds of those who had willed them, if the sleep of the Prince could be achieved. Who could know through what channels the present long peace in the Empire had been granted?

She was aware, however, that George could also decide never to wake: many deaths had been heroic, fully conscious decisions made on the invisible shore as final attempts at holding back life that trickled inexorably away. Perhaps George was at this moment, as he slept, struggling with a strength he had never shown, fighting and defeating the dragons awakened and aroused in the wait. Not even she, not even her love could help him, because she was obliged to act from the side that he had abandoned. The ground of that fight could be as silent as the sea, the pale field of battle they had gazed at under the light of the moon for one whole night together in Livadia; the struggle would be below the shimmering surface, in the depths. And if George were to decide not to wake, someone, centuries later, might carry around with him along the streets of a Russian city the same restlessness and insatiability, the doubt that he had not enjoyed as much as fate had decreed. Because sometimes a generation is not enough to atone, to unravel the tangle of powers waiting to be harmonized, to allow inroads to be made in the more natural laws of a civilization. And at that point violence and murder might seem the only outlet for the guilt that was no one's and that would wander through the centuries waiting to alight on whoever would absorb it in its fullness. The dead are called dead and nothing is known of them after they have been dismissed with that word. She could not lower herself into that sleep; she could wander the breadth of the world, look for that door everywhere, but she could not enter it. There was no power on earth that could open the door into the solitude of that sleep.

She began to convince herself then that George had dwelt within that sleep before, though she had never realized it, conjured up as she had been, by him, as the most beautiful of his dreams. She reached the point of doubting her own existence: her physical presence in the room was no proof. Where was she? From where, within that dimension that man measures in years, had she come summoned by him? She was afraid to turn and witness the slow vanishing of the world, first one wall, then the lights of the village, then the air of that dark night, all gone after George's decision to kidnap her for the other side. They say men are free and do not know it. The only shadow of freedom is sleep and dream.

She must be ready for anything, even the illusion of seeing him waken and call her if, to distract her from his escape he were to decide to take the time even while he fled. The other, the one she had held in her arms, could have warned her by this awakening that he had not made it, had lost the bet. But it was also possible that he was calling her from beyond that sleep, with such desperate cries that centuries of terror had been summoned and monsters awakened that had lain in the conscience of man. She knew of his terror of seeming dead when asleep. His obsession with mirrors was another manifestation of this fear: once he had asked that all the mirrors in the house be smashed when he was dead, that he might turn and rise like Lazarus, called back to the real world by the savor of things she would list for him. This was why things were named, to remind men who are tired of living of certain summer evenings, some dawns after love, the wine of friendship, the joy of some arrivals, some departures, the few memories that can really arouse them, give them the gift of homesickness for this earth. Only she knew in which spots of the garden in Livadia, at Tsarskoe Selo, their intimacy had never been sweeter, the morning most troubling, the eye most reluctant to stop looking and already wet with regret. Only she could name them. To arise was everyone's destiny, but for what further destiny was a personal and secret passion that only a woman could invent, and only once in the life of a man.

He had always been afraid of dying: he wanted her near to teach him how. A mother does this naturally, by preceding the child into death, but George had wanted to rush ahead, letting go of his mother's hand, and it was up to her to take his hand and lead him. It was clear to her now that George was withdrawing from the future because he had already seen it; he had been where it is not possible to be twice, the first time to gather strength for what was to come. All his life now was concentrated in the eyes that looked intently into the century he had not wanted to enter, and, like a river that can run underground the whole breadth of a nation and reappear young and fresh though burdened with windings and falls, George was preparing to vanish.

Helen had no doubt now about what George wanted her to do. She rose and in a flash, as she took the revolver from the halter of George's uniform, she saw their children begging to go on playing a little longer before coming in for the night; she saw herself and him grow old in Cannes, in the villa that the illness could not reach, receiving letters from a Russia so profoundly changed they could never wish to return to it. She kissed his lips, saw him as he had always been and shot him in the temple. The discharge echoed as if he had been fired at many times before.

Only the windows that reflected the white outline of the Elbrus trembled a little.

A NOTE ABOUT THE AUTHOR

Roberto Pazzi was born in Ameglia (La Spezia) in 1946, but has lived in Ferrara for many years. He has had published several poetry collections and novels. The first of these to be translated into English was *Searching for the Emperor* (1988). In addition, he is a literary critic for *Corriere della Sera*.

A NOTE ON THE TYPE

The text of this book was set in Cloister, designed for
American Typefounders c. 1897 by Morris Fuler Benton. It is
one of the early attempts to redesign Jenson's original roman
for modern use. The italic, for which Jenson supplied no
model, was based on older Renaissance Chancery hands.

Composed by Crane Typesetting Service, Inc.
West Barnstable, Massachusetts
Printed and bound by Fairfield Graphics,
Fairfield, Pennsylvania
Designed by Virginia Tan